DRAWING FOR

GOLD

CLARK GUIRE

Book Cover by Garn Yarn

Evobe Field Illustration by Anca Chiosea

Edited by Ramona Mihai

First edition 2025

ISBN: 978-1-7358648-4-6(Paperback)

ISBN: 978-1-7358648-5-3(E-book)

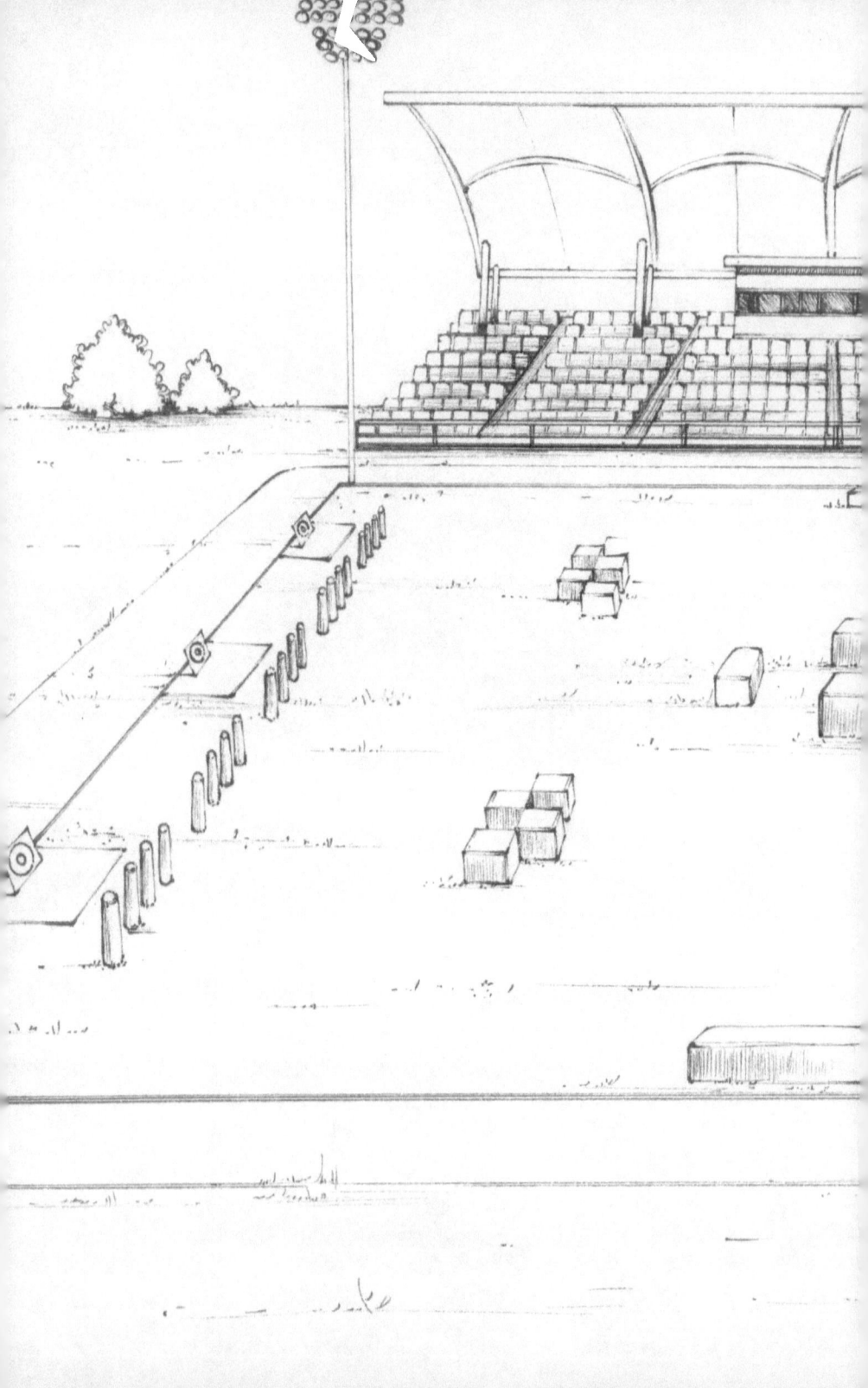

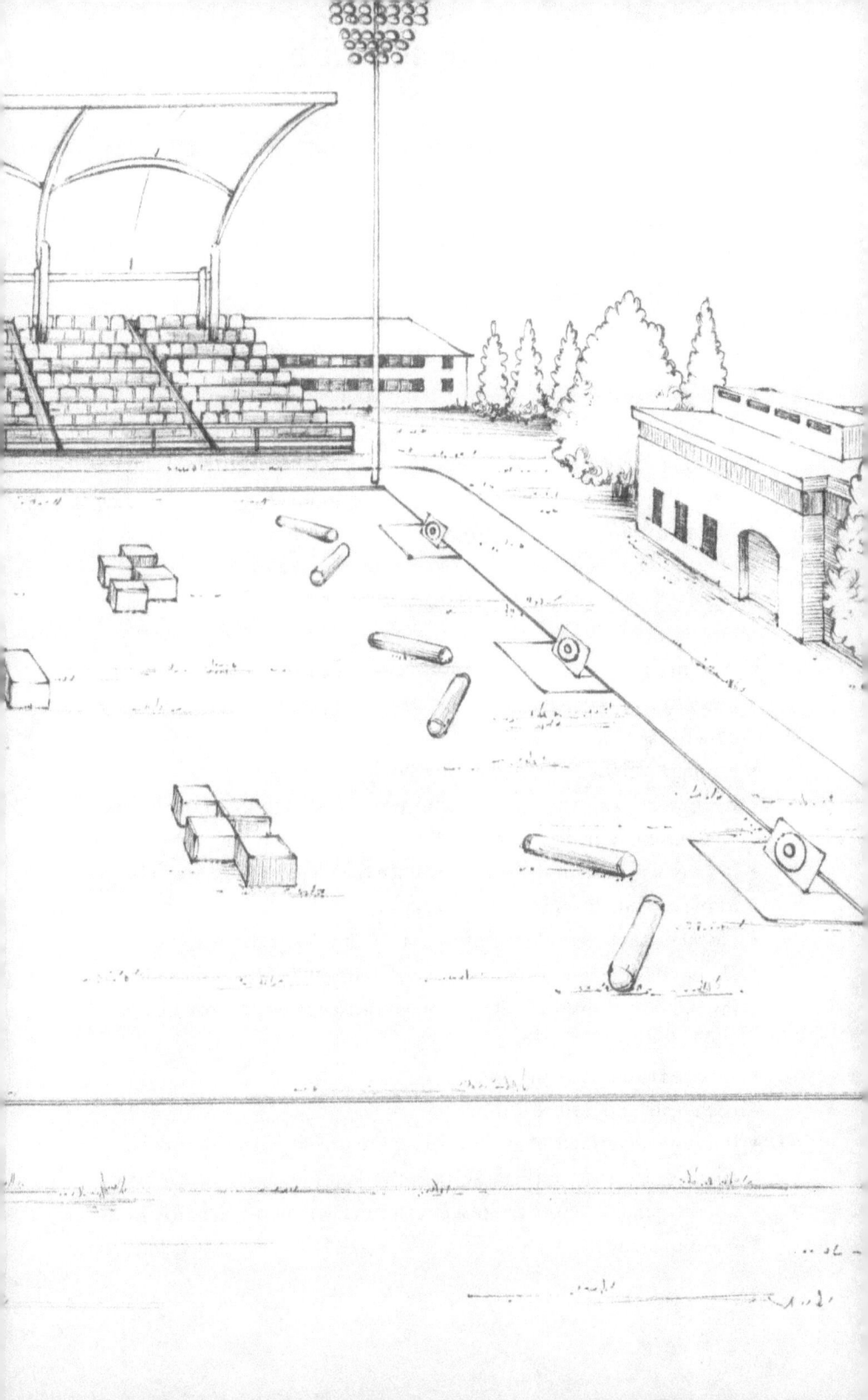

EVOBE RULES

The Game
- The object of the game is to score the most points in a timed match.
- A match consists of 3 periods.
- A period is 20 minutes in length.
- Each team gets 3 timeouts.

Coin toss/Opening rush
- There are two sides of the field, Angled side and Row side. Each side has a different set of bunkers. A coin will be tossed at the beginning of the game, home team calls it. Winner chooses which side to start and end on.
- Runners stand between the blocker boxes before game start. With referee signal, runners rush forward and play begins.

Players
- A team consists of 7 players. 4 runners and 3 blockers.
- Blockers are designated to a blocker box, there are 3 blocker boxes on either side of the field.
- Runners cannot enter the blocker box.
- If a runner gains any points from a target and they are in the blocker box, the amount they gained will be deducted from their total points.
- If a runner causes blocker interference then a penalty shot will be given to the offended team.
- Blockers can use shield on either arm at any point through the game.
- No physical contact between players on opposite teams. (Accidental run ins will be reviewed by referees, if contact deemed purposeful a penalty will be called.)
- No head shots - penalty given.
- Each team gets 5 substitutions per game.
- If a runner runs out of arrows before the period is over they must be taken off the field. Either a substitution must be made or take a one-minute penalty before the player can run back on the field with a new set of 10 arrows.

EVOBE RULES (CONT.)

Points

- Points are awarded for "hits" 1 point when an opponent is hit with an arrow, 10 points (center ring), 5 points (middle ring) and 3 points (outer ring) can be rewarded.
- If there is a tie at the end of regulation 5 minutes over time will be called. Blockers will leave the field and it will be between the runners to gain points. In overtime arrows are no longer dead, they may be picked up and reshot.
- If it still ends in a tie it becomes a shoot out and they will get a chance to hit the target. No matter where a player may hit the target it is only worth 1 point in shootouts.

Boundaries

- Blocker boxes are outlined in paint. Penalties will be given to Runners who step into a blocker box.
- If a point is taken when a runner is outside of the field boundaries, point doesn't count.

Penalties

- Penalty One - Free shot against blockers. Runners stand by the center bunker while 30 second timer is started for penalty. If a shot isn't taken then game resumes at the end of 30 seconds.
- Penalty Two - player is taken off the field for 3 minutes. (Headshots, purposeful body contact)

Equipment and uniform

- No crossbows.
- Helmets must be worn at all times during game play.
- Each runner gets 10 arrows per period.
- Arrows cannot be shared among teammates.
- After an arrow is shot it becomes a dead arrow and cannot be picked up to use until the period is over.
- Player's hit cannot remove paint on uniform until period is over.

CONTENTS

1: ACCEPTANCE

Roman's hands shook; anxiety bubbled in his veins. Joss's honeyed laugh yanked him from the edge of an anxiety attack. Their future rode on which colleges accepted them. Joss wanted them both to go to Georgia, but Roman wanted to go to Pennsylvania; he had already been accepted. If he got into Georgia as well, he wasn't sure he could tell Joss he didn't want to go.

"I got accepted," Joss announced.

Joss grabbed Roman's shoulders, and for a moment Roman caught his reflection in Joss's hazel eyes before being shaken back and forth. A faint scent wafted in the air that always reminded him of Joss—a woodsy orange. Then Joss released him, and Roman collapsed onto the bed, lying in a daze as he stared at the ceiling.

Roman hadn't been able to get himself to check his own results. His screen remained on in his hand. Joss tugged Roman's phone out of his fingers, checking the results himself.

"Damn," Joss groaned. "I was hoping we would go together." The phone landed face down on the bed next to Roman's hip.

Roman smiled sadly at the ceiling. A sense of loss mixed with the feeling of excitement—he was going to his dream school, but he wouldn't be going to the same school as Joss. He saw Joss nearly every day when he wasn't on vacation with his family. They had been through little things they would forget in ten years and big things they would never forget for the rest of their lives. They discovered their sexuality together. Joss's type was everyone; and Roman's type was no one.

"It's okay. I got accepted to the Capybaras." It was reassuring. They were both going exactly where they wanted to, but dread ate at the happiness.

Joss slapped Roman's knees and then squeezed them. "We need to celebrate." Joss pulled away, grabbing his phone. "Something new, something different, you know?"

Roman didn't know. "Like where?"

They always went to Pizza Grove for everything, from celebrations to Joss's fleeting heartaches, which usually disappeared by the second slice of pizza.

Joss shrugged his broad shoulders. "Somewhere nice."

Roman sat up on his elbows.

"I found a place. But we'll have to stop at your house."

It never took Joss long to decide anything. Once Joss saw something he liked, he went for it.

"Why?" Roman asked.

"Because it's fancy."

"Do we have to?" He didn't own fancy clothes, a few decent outfits, but nothing fancy. "I don't have clothes to wear."

"Do you think if you wear my clothes, people would think I'm taking my kid out for dinner?"

Roman rolled his eyes. Maybe the distance would be a good thing. Then he didn't have to hear Joss's stupid jokes. They had been friends since they were kids, through the awkward phases of middle school and the clique separation of high school.

"Come on, what about the clothes you wore for that job before the studio? They were sorta fancy. It'll be fun, and we never do anything like this. This is our first step into the real world." Joss's head tilted to the side with a slight pout on his lips.

Roman forgot about those clothes. He was surprised Joss remembered them. "Fine."

As much as he wanted to complain about Joss, he would miss this. Soon they would be in different states, on opposing teams, only seeing each other a few times throughout the year. Joss was a near constant in his daily life, and soon he would be alone.

Joss tossed his ratty tank top onto Roman's face. Roman tugged it off, shooting a mock glare before tossing it back. Joss batted it away, flexing and posing.

"Best blocker in the world."

Roman rolled his eyes and dropped back onto the bed. Joss was well muscled and attractive to many, but he wasn't the best blocker. That title belonged to Demi Knight, Joss's soon-to-be teammate, who according to Joss, was just at good-looking as himself. Despite his apparent narcissism, Joss had no particular type; he liked humans in general, as long as they were older than him.

Joss buttoned up a black shirt and pulled black slacks over thick, muscled thighs. He used to wish for a body like Joss's. Roman was several inches shorter and thinner. Even when he tried to build muscle, his body remained lean. When he was younger, he wanted to play hockey, but his mom told him he was too small for contact sports. Now he played evobe, a game where players shot each other with foam-tipped arrows.

After Joss dressed, Joss drove them to Roman's house. It was a two-story cut and copy house he had seen on every residential street he had ever driven on. With coral rock instead of lush green grass for a yard. Roman moved quickly, rushing in, tossing his clothes into the laundry basket and rifling through drawers of plain T-shirts, jeans, and shorts for an old grey button-up and a pair of khakis that fit snugly around his thighs. It had been over a year since he last wore them.

The restaurant was a dark wooden building that looked more at home in a deep, whimsical forest than in the middle of a city. The rich wood continued inside, filling the space with a subtle smoky scent. Minimalist chandeliers hung overhead, casting pools of light over each table and creating an intimate atmosphere. Toward the back, an open kitchen revealed chefs in crisp white jackets bustling back and forth.

The petite host led them to a table in the middle of the room. They chose chairs across from each other. Roman straightened the pristine white tablecloth. Soft music played, blending gently with the murmur of conversations from other guests.

Roman lifted the silverware wrapped in a burgundy fabric napkin. He felt like a child pretending to be an adult.

"After graduation, I'm heading to Pennsylvania," Roman said quietly, afraid of being too loud.

Joss leaned forward, his wandering gaze focused on Roman. "Lucky, the Dragons don't start training until August."

Roman didn't fight the smile creeping on his face.

"You're so happy it's obnoxious." Joss wore a soft smile, he wasn't really upset.

"Should I be sad?" Roman set the silverware down.

Joss half shrugged. "Maybe a little. You aren't going to miss me?"

"Of course I am, but you'll probably be too busy to notice." Joss was someone who didn't like to be alone. But he also wasn't committed to relationships, instead he sought out bedmates. It was something Roman didn't understand but he also didn't judge him for. Joss was happy, that was what mattered.

Joss ignored the comment. "I was hoping we'd still be teammates."

Roman fiddled with the edge of the tablecloth. A part of him wanted that too, but a bigger part wanted to be on his own. Wanted to take that leap into being an adult by himself, even if his anxiety sat in the pit of his stomach, coiled like a snake waiting to strike.

"I'll call and keep you updated on all of my hookups," Roman joked. He wouldn't have any, he didn't plan on seeking out people the way Joss did.

Joss grinned, shifting the topic. "Do you want me to pick you up before graduation, or are you going with your parents?"

Graduation was still a few days away, but classes had already officially ended. "Can you pick me up?"

"Yeah. My mom is going to drive later. She said she doesn't want to be there too early. We can all go out to eat afterward. If your parents are cool with it."

"They aren't going."

"What?" Joss's jovial face creased in shock and slid into annoyance as he sat back in his chair.

He hadn't planned to tell Joss, but it wasn't exactly a secret either. Eventually, he would find out. "They're going to Maelie's dance recital." He hated to admit that his parents chose his sister over him, it wasn't the first time, and it wouldn't be the last. But it still stung all the same.

"How is graduation and a stupid recital the same?"

Roman smiled. It was small, but he always enjoyed when Joss got angry on his behalf. "It's always been like this, hoping for it to be different won't actually change it." Joss's anger made it easier for him to swallow his disappointment.

"Still, they could split up at the very least."

"And have one of them miss their special princess dance like an uncoordinated duck on stage?"

Joss laughed. "Your parents are bullshit. It's graduation. They should be legally obligated to go."

They didn't even feel morally obligated to go. "It's whatever. To them, graduation is normal, something that should happen. Maybe college will be different."

Joss shook his head, leaning forward on the table. "It's bullshit, but they're the ones who are going to regret pushing you aside when Maelie goes off and does her own shit. Because who is going to take care of them when they get old and sick? It sure as fuck won't be her and it sure as fuck shouldn't be you. You don't owe them shit."

Roman glanced around to see if anyone was staring at them from all of Joss's swearing, but everyone was in their little bubbles.

His sister was only fourteen, but already felt like the world owed her everything. As long as she continued to *take take take* his parents would always *give give give*. She was the epitome of selfish, and he wasn't sure when or if she would ever grow out of it. He already knew his parents would never want to burden her; it would fall to Roman. He was the older brother. He was the one who was supposed to make sure she continued to have the perfect life, if his parents couldn't do it.

"I know," Roman said, but he knew that if they ever needed him, he wouldn't turn his back on them. He didn't blame his parents for favoring his sister. He had never been good enough for them. It didn't stop him from being disappointed every time he was reminded of it. He spent the night at Joss's. It was the last sleepover for who knew how long.

He came home the next afternoon. Kicking his shoes off at the door, he found several extra pairs, which meant Maelie had friends over. He rushed upstairs to his room, hoping to avoid them.

Roman stared at the missing glass orbs on his desk. Standing up, he walked over to the closet finding more missing glass sculptures. Shaking his head, he stepped back until he could flop on the bed. *Fuck it.* He was going to be leaving soon. His sister could take whatever she wanted. It wasn't like his parents would do anything about it. They never have before.

He waited until after he heard his sister and her friends go downstairs for dinner. He could smell the scent of delivery pizza wafting up the stairs. After their footsteps pounded up the stairs and Maelie's door shut, he left his room.

He looked around the spotless kitchen; every trace of dinner had been cleared away. He tugged open the fridge and retrieved the Tupperware holding three cold slices of cheese pizza. Leaning against the counter, he took a bite of the first slice. He could hear his parents talking in the garage. Hearing his name, he pushed off of the counter, stepping in the hallway between the kitchen and garage.

"She needs more space. I was thinking about turning Romy's room into a studio for her. He's heading off for college, and he can stay in a hotel for visits," his mom said.

His dad responded, "I'll make some calls and see what we can do. When is he leaving?"

"He hasn't said anything to me. Do we have the money to get it done soon? We have trips planned this summer."

"We have that extra savings account."

A few totes dropped on the ground and slid on the cement floor. Roman took a step closer to the garage door.

"Romy's college account?" his mom asked.

"He should be getting scholarships. We've already used some of the money for Maelie's birthday trip this year. He'll be fine."

Roman shook his head. It was so easy for them to just dismiss him, to give away everything meant for him. He shouldn't be surprised, but he continued to hope something would change.

"You're right, he'll figure it out."

Roman threw away the crust he had just bitten into and put the rest of the pizza back in the fridge. His appetite instantly evaporated. His sock-clad feet pounded up the stairs. If they were going to get rid of his stuff anyway, he might as well give them a head start. He grabbed an empty box, sliding his hand along the shelf until all of his glass sculptures his sister hadn't stolen crashed into the box, smashing and breaking against each other. Each one that dropped was like tension releasing from his body. There was no point in leaving them behind. Maelie would steal them when he was gone.

After he was done, adding in old things he didn't need anymore onto the broken shards, he dropped the box off at the curb next to the trash can.

His parents weren't going to change. They would never love him the way they loved his sister. He would leave for Pennsylvania and never move back. Maybe they wanted him to just disappear, or maybe they would miss him. He hoped they would miss him.

Graduation came and went. Roman ignored the pitying looks from Joss's mom and the fact that they got ice cream afterwards, like they were kids again. It was nice, and something he needed before he left for Pennsylvania.

2: PENNSYLVANIA

Jax Tate—captain of the Capybaras—was five feet and four inches full of information. His loose brown curls and light blue eyes reflected a softness that didn't translate to his mouth. He didn't stutter and spoke as quickly as he walked—fast.

"This is the main door." Jax led them into the four-story gray dorm building. "There is a package slot there. Packages will come in through the second door in here." He brought them through the double doors of the building. "You'll need your key card to get into the dorms, and you'll have your own personal key for your dorm room."

"The first room here is the common room." They passed by so quickly he barely glanced over before they were passing it. "Rooms on the right start with one, then go to four. After room four is the first bathroom, then the kitchen." Jax's arms stretched out in both directions. "Rooms on the left start from five and go to thirteen, then the second bathroom and rooms fourteen and fifteen. Rooms are the same as your jersey numbers." Jax spun around and faced them as he walked backwards.

"Morcilla is eleven." Mariona Morcilla had dark wavy hair, dark eyes with unnaturally long eyelashes and full red lips.

"Singh is ten." Haijun Singh kept her head down and her arms crossed.

"Wade is nine. Both bathrooms are available for everyone, both have showers. Clean up after yourself, be respectful of other people's stuff." Jax lifted his phone, not missing a single syllable as he typed. "There are packets of information and your uniforms are in your room. If you have questions, text me. This concludes our tour."

"Are you in a hurry?" Morcilla asked in an annoyed tone.

"Yes, I am. Sorry, I don't want to rush this, but this is all there is. There's really not much to tell you. Also, others are around and you can ask them anything. We're good? Yes? Questions? None?" He nodded and rushed past them.

The three of them stood in the empty hallway, watching each other for a moment. Morcilla left first. Haijun Singh didn't hesitate to copy her and headed to her own room.

Roman stood alone in the hallway. His fingers fidgeted, feeling like a lost child. He shuffled to his room. The door was unlocked, and next to the door frame were black numbers. He set his bag just inside of the door. It was smaller than he was expecting, with light gray walls and a simple white wardrobe on the left, a white desk at the window across from the door and a twin bed on the right, and a single shelf in place of a nightstand. There wasn't much room for anything else. It took him three steps to get across the room in any direction.

He glanced at the packet on the desk and the still-packaged toiletries and bedding. He shoved his bag further in, grabbed his ID card that tripled as his food, bus, and key card for the outer dorm door.

Leaving his room, he headed out to explore the campus. Pennsylvania was warm and humid, a contrast to the heat and dry air of Arizona. Trees were lush with green foliage and bright blooming flowers.

A couple sat at a picnic table in the center of a courtyard surrounded by various dorm buildings. Following the path, he passed by several buildings and reached a line of lit-up vending machines. He slowed down as he passed them. They held various types of food he had never seen in a vending machine before, like ramen and curry, and it came out cooked.

Continuing through the campus, he found different vending machines. He chose a mint green package. Pulling it out, he got a closer look, and it was a peach mint flavored chocolate bar.

Opening it, he didn't hesitate to bite in; he grinned at the flavor. There was no overwhelming flavor of mint or peach; instead, the flavors complemented the chocolate. It was something he had never had before. But being somewhere new, it was the perfect time to try something new. He bought two more and continued exploring. He spent most of the afternoon exploring before making his way back to the dorms.

"Hey, newbs, we're gonna do dinner as a team at six." Lara had pink lips that seemed to sit in a permanent smile. Her dark blue eyes crinkled at the corners.

He frowned, his brows creasing. "Are all the freshmen called newbs? If we are, that might get a little confusing."

Lara laughed. "What's your name?"

"Roman," he told her.

"Last name?" she prompted.

"Wade."

"Middle name?"

His eyes narrowed. "Why?"

Lara smiled, stepping closer to him. "Just seeing if you would offer it up without asking why. So, Rade, I'm Lara Leisel Lamb. A lot of people make the mistake of mixing up the first letter of my name with the first letter of my last name. So I do it too."

"But they both start with an L," he said. He didn't understand her thinking at all. The letters couldn't be switched up, because they were the same letter. Was he being hazed? Was this hazing? He didn't think it was.

"Right? You would think a mistake like that is impossible." She sighed dramatically. "But unfortunately, it's a burden I must bear." She held a hand to her chest.

"So you do that to everyone?"

"Yep!" she said confidently.

He was trying to follow her logic, but it didn't even follow the simple rule she set. "But you used my last name."

"So you're saying I should go around calling you woman?"

"Ah."

"I'm not trying to bully you." She winked and stepped back. "I have to finish getting ready, remember we're meeting at five."

"You said six before," Roman said.

"I like you, Rade."

Lara twirled in a half circle and went back into the bathroom, where there was the sound of water running, clothes rustling, and the murmur of conversation. A popular upbeat pop song started playing. Roman opened his door and shut it behind him. He still had over an hour before he had to go to dinner.

He saved the numbers on his phone, scanned over the other documents and schedules. They had a promo shoot the next day, where they would have to wear their uniforms and take photos. Roman pulled out his uniforms and carefully hung them up. Gingerly, he pressed his hand down on the plastic, straightening the wrinkles. He put away the rest of his dismal amount of clothes. By the time he finished, there were ten minutes until they were supposed to go to dinner.

Through his door he could hear a few laughs, jokes and roughhousing. He waited until it quieted down to slip out of his room and to the bathroom.

The team was spread around the common room when he stepped in. Mariona was laughing with Lara and Natya Thongsuk. Haijun was reading in an armchair without a care to the noise around her, her bag was set on the edge of a long coffee table in front of her. Roman sat in the armchair next to her as they waited. There was a TV mounted on the wall, playing some old show. The volume was low, creating a hum of background noise. The TV was connected to cables attached to several consoles on a TV stand.

Jax clapped his hands together. "Let's head out. We're going to BB's Burgers. It's close, cheap and has a table big enough for all of us. It's just us; the rest won't be coming til later or tomorrow."

Dinner passed in a blur of thick, greasy burgers with playful names, crisp fries, and sharp-tasting beer. Roman accepted the drinks handed to him and went along with the group. He knew he should have waited to eat before downing the first round, but it was already too late. By the time the food arrived, he was halfway through his second beer, and with nothing but sweets in his stomach all day, it hit him quickly.

He slid the beer away and drank water as he ate. An uneasiness settled in his stomach. He wasn't much of a drinker. A few parties and drinks with Joss didn't equate to keeping up with the speed of college students. The conversations were a blur of noise he couldn't decipher. He panicked between a bite of his burger and three fries. His leg constantly bounced under the table as he continued to eat, unable to stop himself. Another drink of water and he slowly calmed down; everything was just new. Nothing here felt familiar. He tugged out his phone and texted Joss.

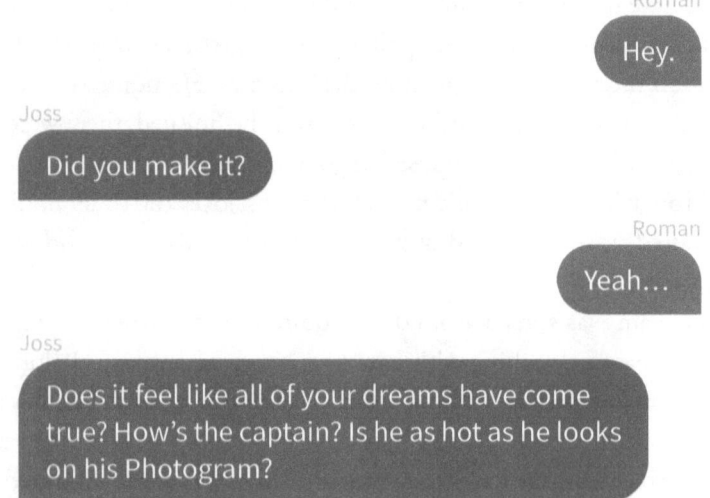

Roman

Hey.

Joss

Did you make it?

Roman

Yeah…

Joss

Does it feel like all of your dreams have come true? How's the captain? Is he as hot as he looks on his Photogram?

Roman's shoulders relaxed, his foot stopped bouncing and the unsettling feeling evaporated. He shook his head, of course Joss would ask that.

Roman

He looks the same as his photos.

Joss

So he's pretty hot, what about the others?

Roman

I don't know.

Joss

Sigh. I thought you cared about my sex life.

Roman

You think I care about your sex life?

Joss

You don't? What kind of friend are you?

Roman

Your best friend.

Joss

And you better not forget it.

Roman put away his phone. *Forget Joss? Impossible.*

3: PROMO

Roman woke up slowly, reorienting himself to his surroundings. Light streamed in from the window, causing him to squint. His alarm sounded two hours early so he could shower without worrying about being in anyone's way. Grabbing his stuff, he shuffled to the empty bathroom.

Light blue tiles reflected around the square stall from the white overhead light. The color reminded him of the turquoise from Arizona, from home. He hung his towel on the hook attached to the door and turned the lock behind him. Roman placed his own spicy citrus-scented, blood orange-colored bottles on the empty bottom shelf. He turned the handle and jumped when cold water sprayed him. Goosebumps covered his body as he scrambled to adjust the temperature.

"Coach said we have to be there early with our hair and makeup already done."

"I don't think she understands what touch-ups are."

Roman's sudsy hands paused in his hair as he heard the girls in the bathroom. In high school, they separated the locker rooms. As fast as he could, he rinsed off the soap and finished washing. Only when he was certain the room was empty did he step out of the stall, wrapped in his gray towel. In the hallway, he pretended he didn't see half of the team milling around and rushed without running to his room. He knew he would get used to sharing with the girls, but for now he would wake up earlier when he was sure no one would go into the bathroom when he wanted to shower.

The first part of the photo shoot, they wore their white long-sleeved uniforms, with a dark pink logo and dark pink pants. The second half was dark pink, with a light pink logo and light pink pants. He traced the dark pink collar, then the stripe from the shoulder that curved down the bicep and down to the back of the arm to the elbow. A dark pink stripe started from the armpit to the bottom of the shirt. His name and number were in dark pink on the back and the Capybaras logo across his chest on the front with *Harmony* written above the logo and *Capybaras* below it. The pants and socks were the same dark pink with two thin lines on the sides.

A photo studio was set up at their practice field, in a large building on the other side of the campus from their dorm. After he put his uniform on, he never wanted to take it off. It was one of his biggest motivators when choosing Pennsylvania for a school.

They lined up according to their jersey numbers putting Jax in front of him. He twisted his fingers as he watched the seniors model like pros. He tried to remember their poses. In family photos, he was usually the one on the edge, hands shoved in his pockets or hanging stiffly at his sides. When Joss snapped selfies, all he managed was a simple smile. As his turn approached, the anxiety had his ears ringing. He couldn't hear a word the photographer said. His smile was weird, and his breathing was short. He quickly left after he saw the flash three times. *Photoshop could fix anything, right?* When the photos came out, he only glanced at his own before he pretended they never existed. The only thing he liked was the uniform.

"You don't have to be so stiff taking the photos," Jax said.

Roman looked up after adjusting his uniform.

"I know it seems serious, but it's not a big deal. Before we all leave, they're going to go through the photos and call out the people who need to retake them. It's better to just relax, have fun and don't worry about it than hang around here until they're satisfied."

If his anxiety was a switch Roman could turn off, he would have shut it off and ripped it from the wall. Taking a few deep breaths, he tried to think of it as Joss taking photos when he would use Roman as a stand-in for himself. He would have Roman stand in a certain position and throw out a few poses, and then they would trade places. He bumped into Jax's back, mumbled a sorry and took a step back. Now he was wondering if Joss only did that so Roman wouldn't feel awkward.

When he passed through the second round of photos, he got a thumbs up from Jax. He was forced to stay for one round of extra photos for the light jersey before he could leave. Cameron and Pio had to stay behind as well for messing around too much in the photos.

"We can't all be like Dae and Lara," Cameron said, he flipped back pretend hair. He was tall, with neatly trimmed black hair. Pio's dark skin stood out against the photographer's background. He posed dramatically, causing Cameron to laugh.

Daehyun Park walked in scrolling through his phone. He looked as if a meticulous sculptor created him. From the way his hair held a slight flip, to his strong cheekbones and his long legs. He was the kind of person that didn't exist outside of magazines or a runway show.

"Knock it off," Coach called out. "Park, you're late!"

Pio and Cameron both straightened up and finished their photos in record time. Dae slipped in front of Roman. "I'll be quick," he told him in a smooth, deep voice. Roman nodded, unable to speak, allowing him to take his place in line.

Roman was the last one to take his photos. The photographer was quick, guiding him a few times before letting him leave.

He decided to not change out of the uniform and instead wear it for the rest of the day. When he left the building, he realized everyone had already left. On the way there, he just jumped in the car that had an empty seat. He was so nervous about the photoshoot he didn't even know whose car it was.

Tugging his phone out of his pocket, he pulled up the GPS and started walking. After crossing the street, his phone couldn't find the GPS location. He kept walking and resetting the app before he finally saw the dorm building in the distance. It was already noon, and his stomach grumbled. He looked around but didn't know where to go to eat. Until he thought of the vending machines and all the types of ramen they offered. He grinned, now he knew exactly what to do for lunch. Changing direction, he headed for the vending machines instead of the dorm.

Steam billowed from the top of his ramen, carrying a fresh beef scent, making his mouth water. He used the chopsticks and lifted several noodles into his mouth. Flavorful spices filled his mouth. He quickly took several more bites and lifted the bowl to drink the broth, causing his body to fill with warmth. His body relaxed with each bite. Pennsylvania wasn't quite what he thought it would be, but it was new.

4: PRACTICE

Roman stared at what looked like a padded, wooden torture chamber on the side of their practice field.

"That's the secret to us being the best dodgers in the league," Jax said, his head tilted toward the mechanism.

They weren't the best dodgers in the league. They were the second best, though.

Three thunderous claps gained the team's attention. "Gather round," Harper Greer, the coach, called out.

Coach Greer was a woman with a firm presence and a stern face. Bristol Fortin, the assistant coach, stood next to her. She looked like the sweet to her savory; she smiled gently with a clipboard in her hands.

The coach spoke. "We're going to get right into it. I assume you've read the packets and know who to talk to about what. I want half of you in the weight room, the other half with the dodger, switch and then we'll scrimmage.

"Let's not waste time with unnecessary chit chat, so I'll keep this short. I want to talk about the traits that make a good team. Individual progress is how the team progresses. If one member is weak, then the team is weak. You can't rely on others to be strong for you; you need to be strong by yourself. We are here to guide you, not babysit you. I expect you all to act as adults and work hard."

Assistant Coach Fortin spoke up. "We have a switch-up this year. Yueying Ling will be a blocker starting this season."

"As for our new players, Wade and Singh, are runners, and Morcilla is a blocker. Now we can start practicing. Jax, can you separate the team?"

Jax jumped up, splitting them down the middle. Roman had to stay with the dodger.

Natya gave him a half-smile and patted him on the shoulder. "Don't worry, you only bruise a little. It's fun when you get used to it."

He didn't want to get used to it; he didn't want to get anywhere near the contraption. He could already picture the bruises it would leave, knowing he'd have to suffer through the summer heat in long sleeves just to keep them hidden.

Roman shuffled behind his group toward the other side of the field. Jax leaned against the wooden behemoth, his eyes going around the group, and Roman realized the other two freshmen were also in his group.

Jax patted the contraption as if it were a dog. "The coach's husband is a carpenter; he made it for us. First walk through, get used to the mechanics of it and then run through."

His stomach writhed. On his first step into the wooden contraption, he hit his forehead on the wooden bar. The padding helped, but not by much. Ducking, his right shoulder hit a bar, then his left shin. Over and over, his body slammed into padded wood. As he stumbled out of the wooden chamber, his knees gave way and dropped him to the grass.

Roman watched the others, how they struggled and made it through looking no better than him.

Running through, he only avoided the first bar where he ducked; he was fully stopped at the next bar and then the next until he made it out. He hoped this was a hazing ritual and not part of their regular practice.

He was terrified as he walked toward the weight room that he would find wooden dumbbells. Who knew what else the coach's husband had made for her. Maybe they would use wooden bows and arrows too. Sunlight shined across the practice field from the large skylight adorning the building's roof. Instead, he found a normal weight room. Shuffling forward with a sigh, he chose an empty spot at the ropes to start the first round of circuits. He faced the mirrors as he worked his arms up and down. His eyes caught on Daehyun, who squatted while raising a kettlebell. Roman forced his gaze back onto himself and smoothed out his breathing. Once he focused, it was easy to get lost in the rhythm.

The freshmen—Roman, Haijun, and Mariona—headed over to the gear storage to gather their new gear. He stacked his gear in his arms: armored compression pants, arm pads, chest protectors and knee pads, helmets, wrist guards, quivers and bows. All the players wore armored pads under their uniforms. They gave him four different sets, two in each color. But only two helmets, quivers, and bows. In contrast, blockers got heavier pads and had a padded arm block.

After they geared up, he slung the quiver over his shoulders and took his position at the end of the field. The whistle sounded, and he ran toward the first bunker. He could already hear the coach calling out points. Instead of encouraging him, he found it distracting. He slid along the bunker further into the field and felt an arrow hit his left shoulder. Lara stood on top of a bunker fifteen feet away. She jumped down, narrowly avoiding an arrow. The coach called out his point for the opposite team.

Roman ended the scrimmage with six arrows. Coach Fortin recorded how many arrows they shot, points they got and points taken against them. He glanced around at the other runners and found that they were left with only one or two arrows. Their practice stats were added to a whiteboard as motivation to do better.

The coach clapped her hands. "We'll be meeting every day except the weekends for the summer sessions. This is the time to show us how hard you're willing to work."

Roman got a ride back to the dorms with Jax, Pio, and Cameron. He showered and took a piece of pizza that someone had ordered and offered to the entire team. The rest of the night, he stayed in his dorm.

There was a certain dread in his stomach when they ran drills against the blockers. All the runners started at one end of the field and had ten minutes to get as many points against the blockers as they could. Except every time he pointed his arrow toward Silvana, he knew she was glaring at him. No one would believe him because they all wore helmets and he couldn't see her face, let alone her eyes, but he felt it in his entire body.

His shoulders shifted instinctively and angled toward Morcilla, who drew more attention from others because she was new. He didn't see it that way; she was simply the only option open to him on this side of the field that wasn't Silvana. Weaving through other runners and bunkers, he made his way to the other side of the field and took aim on Yueying. She was the shortest of the three, but she was quick.

After practice he headed out of the building, squinting against the bright sunshine. He had taken to running to and from practice and always showered at the dorms.

Mariona was on the phone walking ahead of him. "Don't even joke. They aren't my friends, they're my teammates. I wouldn't call co-workers friends either. Friends are by choice, and I didn't choose these people. The only okay one is—" She turned her head and glared at Roman as if it was his fault for being there. He quickened his pace, not hearing the rest of her words. She was right; teammates didn't have to be friends. He certainly wasn't going to try to be friends with someone who didn't want to be his friend.

Summers in Pennsylvania were pleasant and nothing like the dry scorching heat of Arizona. He found a path he liked to jog on in the mornings. Once or twice he ran into Daehyun, who didn't acknowledge or glance at him as they passed by each other. He wondered if he had done any advertisements for sport gear because he held a perfect form as he ran.

When he arrived back at the dorm with a light sheen of sweat coating his body, he could immediately hear Pio, Cameron, and Jax roughhousing in the common room. They were always messing around, sometimes at practice the team would get yelled at for not being serious when in actuality it was only a few of them who were playing around.

He hadn't grasped the mentality of their team yet, nor the coach's style of coaching. The coach rewarded them as individuals, but punished them as a team.

On the way to his room, he nearly ran into Silvana coming out of her room. She glanced at him, tossed her hair to the side and continued talking to Yueying who rushed after her.

"If you're too busy to help me then fine, don't help me," Silvana said.

"I will help you. I just need to move some things around," Yueying said, almost as if she was begging. It was strange, and he continued past them, not wanting to know what they were talking about.

The dorm had moments when it was a constant flurry of noise, and other times it felt as if he lived there alone. In a way, it was no different from home. With his sister always having friends over. Except here he couldn't escape to Joss's house. Joss had gotten a summer job to save up as much fun money as possible before he headed to Port Vista. Roman didn't think he could handle getting a job; his anxiety was already pushing the limits of what he could stand.

His only happiness had been the vending machines; trying something new every time gave him something to look forward to. And he needed something to look forward to, something to ease the tension. As soon as he thought he had caught up with the team, they were already far ahead again. Every practice felt like a test, and he was failing. After practice, he would drag his sore body to the team board, where he continued to reign at the bottom. He couldn't surpass anyone, let alone have anyone drop to his level.

The summer drifted by in a repetitive manner of wandering around campus, finding new things to try, spending time in his dorm and struggling through practice.

5: SHATTER

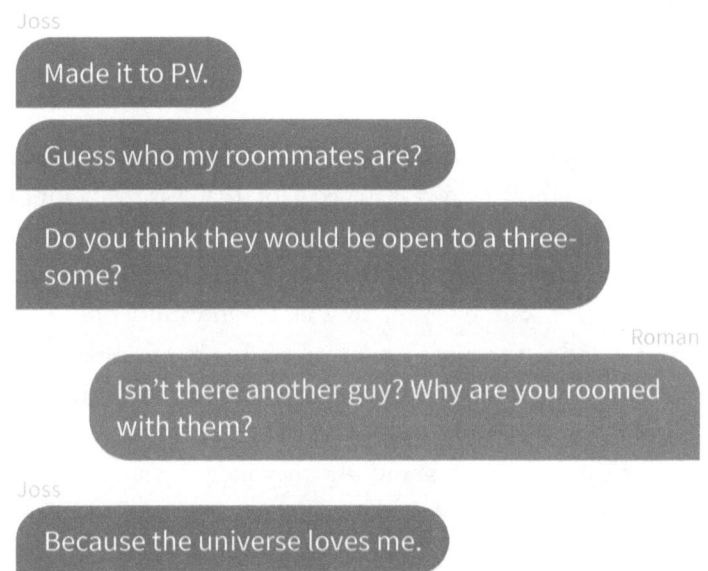

Joss

Made it to P.V.

Guess who my roommates are?

Do you think they would be open to a three-some?

Roman

Isn't there another guy? Why are you roomed with them?

Joss

Because the universe loves me.

He shook his head, the universe did love Joss, why did it feel like it hated him? Maybe they would always balance each other out. Roman's glass blowing class was cancelled because the classes were no longer in session, so instead, he accepted the beginners' drawing class they offered as a replacement. The drawing class was his first class of the semester.

Roman sat near the window, his easel blank in front of him. The harsh morning light scorched his face. The professor asked them to sketch something they had drawn a thousand times before. Roman knew what he was going to sketch. It was going to be a glass orb that he had sketched and made a hundred times before. His hand was quick as he pressed the pencil to the paper, he added a burst of shaded graphite in the center of the orb. It wouldn't win any awards, but he wasn't here to become an award-winning artist.

It took him three minutes to sketch, while the rest of the class took nearly the entire hour. He debated dropping the class; he had already gone against his advisor's suggestion to keep his class load light.

Roman jumped as the teacher spoke next to him. "Explain your piece to me." The teacher was a medium-built woman in a simple blue dress. She stared at his easel as if he drew a puzzle and she was trying to figure out how to put it together.

"Uh, it's a glass orb."

"And what does it represent?"

"A paperweight?" Roman didn't know what she was asking for. It represented something he had sketched a lot; that was the point of the assignment.

"Is everyone done?" she asked the class. Voices sounded around the room in assent. "I want everyone to walk around and write a number between one and ten on the piece of paper, do not affect the drawing, and don't leave your initials. Ten being good and one being bad, you can choose your own criteria to judge it. In the art world, you will have to accept criticism. You won't know why they judged you, just that they did. Someone will always judge your work, just as you will judge theirs."

Roman took his pencil and with the rest of the class they played a morbid game of musical chairs. Roman gave every project a ten, some of his classmates were able to depict the human face, others drew detailed animals. When he returned to his own seat, he saw it filled with ones and a single two. Everyone's sketch showed their passion for drawing, even if it wasn't perfect, a lot of details went into their work. When he looked at his own, he felt nothing. Roman stared at his piece while everyone packed up and headed out of the room. He didn't even want to take it with him.

"I never tell a student to drop out, but I don't think taking an elective you aren't interested in, is wise."

Roman's eyes didn't stray from his artwork. He had just been thinking of dropping the class, but as soon as he was told he should, why did he feel the need to defend his work?

"I'm not an artist," Roman said.

"You are, everyone is. A football player creates a work of art on the football field. A writer creates a work of art with words. Your sketch lacks passion and feelings. It's a three-dimensional drawing with a one-dimensional emotion. You have a few weeks before you need to decide to take or drop the class. Show me your passion for art; draw something real. If you do that, I will give you extra credit points. If you believe it's too difficult or a waste of your time, then drop my class."

Roman didn't leave his seat until the teacher had packed up her things and left the classroom. The pencil cracked under the pressure of his grip. He didn't know why everyone was trying to get rid of him, first his parents and now the teacher; maybe even his coach would eventually kick him off the team. Letting go of the pencil, he twisted his left index finger into his right hand. *No, art was an escape, something free, he could do this, he just had to try harder.*

It took him three days and a weekend to take up the courage and find a glass studio in the next town over, he had to order a ride and make an appointment.

He pushed through the studio's door as a bell chimed above him. The room was colorful with splashes of color on the walls and held various glass sculptures with price tags on black shelves.

"Hello! Welcome to Shatter Studio, how can I help you today?

He cleared his throat. "I uh, have an appointment."

"Let me look." She typed on the computer a few times. "Is it under Wade?"

"Yeah."

"Okay, I have an hour and you wrote you were experienced, could you tell me about it?"

Roman licked his lips. "I used to work in a studio, um, I've been doing it for a few years."

"Sorry, I don't mean for this to sound like an interview. We get quite a few people who say they are experienced and they have never set foot in a hot shop before."

"That can be pretty dangerous."

"It is, the door is right there, all of the tools are marked, if you have any questions, you can ask me at any time."

"Thank you."

Stepping into the hot shop, with the sharp scent of burning paper and smoldering embers, felt surprisingly like a breath of fresh air. *He may not be the best evobe player, son or friend, but he could mold glass and make something worth looking at.* He lifted the finished piece with a smile as it glinted in the light. It was exactly what he pictured in his head and on the sketches he brought with him.

He arrived early at his drawing class on Monday morning. He set the large flame-shaped sculpture on the teacher's desk. From the center bottom, it was light orange, then became dark red and then blue, and at the tip and in the center was a small light green.

His teacher glanced up. "Ah, I thought all of the glass blowing students had dropped my class already."

"I wanted to see what the drawing class was like first," Roman told her.

"It's beautiful, what did you feel when you were making it?"

"Determination, I wanted to prove something I guess, and I enjoy making things."

"May I?" She reached out but didn't touch the sculpture.

"You can have it."

She shook her head, her curls shifted around her head. "Oh, that's not necessary."

Roman shrugged. "I can just throw it away."

"That's really unnecessary. If you insist, I will keep it." She lifted it up, examining it from every angle. "Now I just need to find out how to bring all of the passion you put into here onto paper."

Roman didn't know how she planned on doing that. He went to the seat he had chosen on the first day as other students trickled into the room. By the end of class, he decided to stay, he liked the teacher. He wasn't sure if he would be able to win his teacher's approval, but he liked having something to do when he couldn't work with glass. It cost too much to go to the glass studio in his free time. And he could try to enjoy using a pencil to create instead of fire.

It was warm in late September; the promise of fall weather was still unfulfilled. It was Friday afternoon, and this weekend, they would start having practices on the weekends. Morning practices had already changed to evening as classes started.

His speech class was his least favorite. He sat by himself in the class-room, until a student rushed in at the last second, scanned the filled seats of the room, stopping on the seat next to Roman. Roman tugged his bag closer to himself in a silent invitation.

"Thanks," he whispered with a smile.

He tried to focus, but he recoiled at the idea of public speaking. To keep himself from leaving the classroom, he barely paid attention to the teacher and instead focused on taking notes. As soon as the teacher dismissed them, Roman shoved his things in his bag, ready to run out of the room if he needed to.

He dropped his backpack off in the dorm, grabbed his team duffle bag, and jogged to practice. For a few miles, he could forget about homework, missing Joss, and his parents not reaching out since he left. If he dwelled on it for too long, it felt like a tidal wave waiting to sweep him out to sea. It was easier to ignore the emotions than to deal with them.

The team gathered around the whiteboard.

"Wade, are you paying attention?" the coach called out.

Roman's gaze focused on the coach, nodding.

"You need this more than anyone." She tapped the board with a green marker. "Starting runners are going to focus on these three areas." The coach pointed to the field drawn on the whiteboard.

Shame and guilt swirled in his stomach and throat. His focus remained glued to the board and the coach, vowing to only focus on evobe during practice and games, he wouldn't get distracted again. Even if he had been listening, his gaze had just wandered off for a second.

"I'm not a babysitter. I'm your coach. I need your head in the game at all times. Do you understand?"

"Yes, Coach," the team said in unison.

Roman knew, they all knew that the coach directed the words at him. He swallowed his embarrassment, swallowed his resentment, swallowed his anxiety, and swallowed his feelings of inadequacy. His stomach churned and sloshed with all of it. He fought the nausea and tightened his fists.

"Let's try the first formation; this shouldn't be anything new to you. These are basics that you all should know by now. We only have a month left till the season starts."

Roman followed the rest of the team onto the field. Sliding his helmet over his head, he held his bow and went to the edge of the field. For a moment, where no one could see his face, relief washed over him, but it didn't last long. It never did. The coach was watching him; the team was counting on him, and he needed to be better.

Haijun and Pio were on his team of runners, with Mariona and Silvana as their blockers. Roman hadn't warmed up to them. Everyone was busy with their own things, besides being teammates and living in the same dorm. They didn't interact much.

The whistle blew, and he rushed onto the field, he veered to the left and the whistle blew again. His run slowed, and he turned to the coach.

"Wade! That's the wrong formation!"

Roman clenched his bow tight in his hand. He swore he was supposed to go left.

"It's the outer run. You're supposed to go right," Pio told him as they set up again.

Roman swallowed hard. Shame burned his cheeks and insides. Annoyance tinged Pio's usually jovial voice. Mariona had her arms crossed. He could only imagine the annoyed expression on her face hidden under her helmet.

They set up again. This time he ran to the right, kept to the outer edge and tried to focus on using as many arrows as he could without wasting them. Wasting them got them in more trouble than having any left over. There really wasn't any lower to go. He was already at the bottom of the runner's board. Practice ended without that changing.

Roman shot arrows at the target range. Everyone had already gone back to the dorms. He didn't care how many bullseyes he got. If he couldn't get them in a scrimmage, then they were useless. He had to get better. With a slow breath in, he stared the target down, a slow breath out as he released the arrow. Another bullseye. His parents didn't care about him, his teachers didn't either, and now his coach didn't think he was good enough. He grabbed another arrow, nocked it on the bowstring, and released it. Bullseye. His arm fell to his side, he leaned the bow against the empty bench and grabbed his water, his eyes straying to the team board.

Their names and stats were displayed on long magnetic strips. He could just pull his name from the bottom and stick it to the top. A sardonic smile rose to his face, if only it was that easy.

He thought he would be better by now, he had been practicing since June, the time just slipped through his fingers. No matter how many times he ran through the torture machine or lifted weights or ran formations, he wasn't keeping up. He barely knew the team and now school had started adding to his list of worries.

There was one month left till the evobe season started, he had to at least be able to play. Some teams played all of their players, others only played the starting ones. He didn't know what the coach would choose when the time came. He could only wait.

6: Happy Birthday

Roman woke up on Saturday to a text that practice was cancelled, with only four days until the evobe season started. It was the first time he had ever gotten good news on his birthday. Roman didn't allow the change to interrupt his routine. He tugged on a pink T-shirt and black running shorts to go on his morning run.

Usually, his birthdays comprised of his sister's restaurant of choice and her favorite flavor of cake, strawberry with sprinkles. In a small effort to fix it, Joss and his mom would take him out for ice cream the weekend after. They never said that's why they did it, but he knew it was.

Before his sister was born, he would get birthday pancakes and a chocolate cake, after he changed to wanting lemon cake, his sister protested and his parents adopted the idea of as long as Maelie was happy, everyone was happy. He never complained because he still went out to dinner and got a cake.

A cool breeze made him run faster to keep warm. Clouds blocked out the sun, creating a sunless path. He evened out his breath, breathing through his nose and remained focused on what was in front of him. He kept to his usual route around campus and circled back to the dorm.

With a light sheen of sweat clinging to his body, he opened the dorm building door using his ID card. A few team members milled around the hallway. Jax, Lara, and Daehyun were all sipping on coffee in the kitchen. Pio was singing in the shower, with Cameron chiming in as a background singer.

Roman grabbed his shower bag and chose to go into the empty bathroom. He took a refreshing cold shower, washing away the sweat and cooling his heated body. He loved cold showers after working out, it was soothing. Like ice cream on a hot summer day.

His assignments were finished, and he was left without any plans for the day. Some days blurred together and he struggled to break out of the monotony. He didn't want to stay in his room on his birthday; he also didn't have anyone to spend it with. The team would want to enjoy their rare free day. He didn't want them to feel obligated to hang out with him or to get him anything. Though he was probably thinking too much.

On his way out of the dorm he didn't see anyone else, so he took it as a sign not to say anything. He explored the parts of the campus he hadn't been to yet. It wasn't an exciting thing to do, but he didn't want to spend money to do something by himself. The scholarship was enough to pay for everything and a bit extra, he had some saved from his part-time job while he was still in high school, and he didn't shop unnecessarily.

As long as he was smart with the money, he could survive the next four years without a single penny from his parents, and he would have to, because his parents were spending the money they saved for him on his sister. He knew they didn't owe him the money; he just thought that since they saved it for *him*, then it would be *his*.

The campus was bursting with autumn colors. It was quiet, with a few couples and students milling around. He passed by a small public garden. A fence enclosed the garden, and a tall brick clock tower rose twenty feet beyond it. The wind picked up, scattering colorful leaves across the sidewalk. He shoved his hands in his hoodie pocket. Across the street from campus there was a bakery he had been thinking of going to. Today was the perfect day to try it, spinning on his heel he headed south.

The bakery was bustling with people getting breakfast, bread, snacks, and cupcakes. Roman browsed the assortment of cupcakes, he couldn't find a lemon flavored one, so he settled for a Madagascar vanilla cupcake with brown butter frosting.

The dorm was deserted when he got back. Roman slid a single bone-white birthday candle into the top of the cupcake. Flicking the lighter he lit the candle. He held the cupcake up, watching the flame sway for a few seconds.

"Happy birthday to me," he whispered. Taking a shallow breath, he blew out the candle.

Ten minutes before midnight, Joss called him to wish him a happy birthday. His parents and sister hadn't reached out, but he swallowed the disappointment of being forgotten.

For a nineteenth birthday, it wasn't horrible. Even if nothing great happened, nothing terrible happened either.

7: BIRTHDAY CELEBRATION

"What did you do this weekend?" Lara asked on Monday afternoon.

A storm had started that morning and thunder sounded in the distance. They had only figured out that morning they had the speech class together. They usually sat on opposite sides and hadn't paid much attention to who came or who left. Lara wasn't Joss, but it was nice to have a familiar face in a class.

Roman glanced at the teacher, who was setting up her slideshow. He leaned back in her chair, his gaze sliding to Lara lazily. "Had my birthday."

Lara's eyes widened, and her mouth parted. "You should have told me it was your birthday; we could have celebrated."

Roman shrugged. The teacher who was having technical difficulties. "It's alright, I didn't want to do anything."

"We should still doing something, maybe something small?" Lara said. She set her chin in her hand with her elbow on the table and smiled at him. "Just a birthday hat and cake."

"Maybe, I'll think about it." Roman attempted some kind of enthusiasm but it fell flat.

Lara laughed lightly. "It'll be fun, I promise I won't make a big deal of it."

"Maybe," he responded.

She hummed. "I'll wear you down."

The professor began class, ending the conversation. They went their separate ways for their next class, but in the middle of it, he got a text.

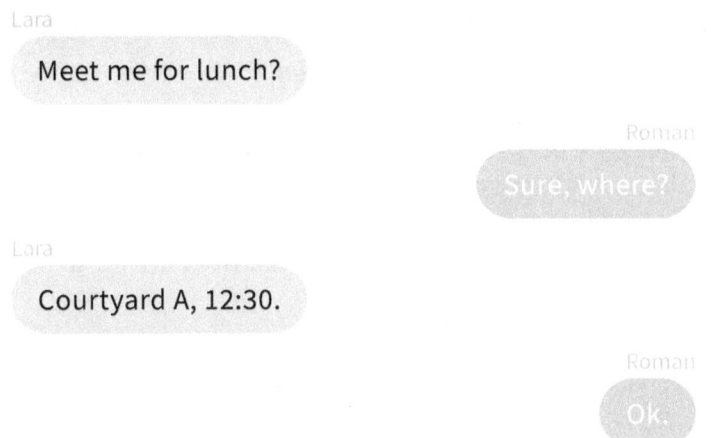

Lara

Meet me for lunch?

Roman

Sure, where?

Lara

Courtyard A, 12:30.

Roman

Ok.

Courtyard A was the courtyard for the dining hall. It was the most popular place to eat on campus because it had a variety of choices. Roman usually preferred something faster and less populated, like the vending machines. There were certain times when there was a line for them, but he had gotten proficient at choosing the right times to go to avoid them.

Lara waved from across the way, half standing on a picnic table. Roman headed toward her weaving through the crowd and avoided people sitting on the ground. Lara already had food in front of her and an extra sandwich.

"I found us a place to sit, I almost had to fight someone for it."

Roman looked around, every table was full. "It's pretty busy."

"Yeah. I got you a sandwich, just turkey and cheese, if that's okay. I grabbed some condiment packets." Lara dumped out a small white bag full of various condiments between them.

"Thanks, it's great. I can pay—"

She waved her hand. "It's a sandwich. Don't worry about it."

His shoulders relaxed, and the tension built up since she told him the spot they were meeting at released. Roman had been avoiding the dining hall. Because it was always so busy, it was nice not to have to go inside. His mind filled with ideas on how to pay her back for her kindness.

"So tell me about yourself? Your birthday is in October and you play evobe, that's all I know," she said, pouring mustard across her own turkey and cheese sandwich.

Roman glanced at his sandwich. He grabbed his own mustard packet from the pile. "There's not much to tell."

Lara chuckled and leaned forward as if they were going to exchange secrets. "There's always something. Are you from here or somewhere else?"

"Arizona."

"See? That's already interesting. I'm from upstate New York."

He didn't think being from there was that interesting, but she made it seem like it was. "That's cool," he said lamely.

Roman thought he would struggle to talk to Lara, but instead of bombarding him with questions, she talked about her own life and friends. Besides being from New York, Lara had an older sister and was working as a model while getting a business degree. He returned the information given to him: he had a younger sister, was unemployed, and was focusing on general classes before focusing on a major.

"I have to head out. We should meet up tomorrow for lunch, if you're free. I have more time tomorrow."

"Yeah, that works for me." Most of his classes were in the morning and afternoons, his lunch time was usually open.

Lara grabbed her trash. With a wave of her hand, she disappeared into the crowd.

That weekend, he finally agreed to celebrate his birthday.

"Please put on something other than our team's gear." Lara had begged. *"I don't care if it's a clown costume."*

Roman stared at his abysmal wardrobe. It was just easier to wear the free clothes the team had given him than buy clothes. He finally found a faded black T-shirt and grabbed a pair of ripped jeans. It was tighter than he usually wore his clothes, but it wasn't too uncomfortable. He could still move around in them, though he had no idea what Lara had planned.

Anxiety wrapped around his body like a tightly wound coil. He liked hanging out with Lara, but sometimes she could be pushy. They met in the hallway where she nodded approvingly, with Natya at her side.

Natya was tall and toned, wearing a black skort and black crop top. Her white liner made her almond eyes look larger. Her long brown hair was in waves over her shoulders.

Lara's long blonde hair was in two buns, with maroon eyeliner highlighting her blue eyes. She wore a blue skirt and a tight white T-shirt.

He couldn't figure out where they were going based on their clothes or makeup. It was casual but also could indicate going out.

"Let's go wreak some havoc, joking, don't look so serious, Rade. We're going to have some pure clean fun."

From Natya's smile, he didn't think anything about it would be pure or clean.

Natya threw a tanned arm over his shoulders. "I already ordered us a ride. Don't you worry about anything; we got it all planned out."

Instead of being calmed down by her words, it only increased the squirming in his stomach and sense of dread.

The car took them across town, every turn and stop light, every building they passed bloomed with a possibility of where they were going. They got out of the car, and Lara's soft hand covered his eyes as she dragged him forward.

A door opened, and her hand fell away. It was a massive indoor playground.

"I told you I would take you somewhere pure and clean; well clean is semantics."

"I don't think that's how that word is used."

She shrugged. "Semantics."

"I really want to go down the slide," Natya said, tugging them toward the counter. They kicked their shoes off, and Lara paid.

The playground looked like someone had taken a children's play area and scaled it up. Adults and teens ran around like kids, even though the sign clearly stated that no one under thirteen was allowed.

"Tag, you're it!" Natya said, slapping his arm as she ran towards the slide. Lara ran in the opposite direction to the rope ladder and large tunnels. He rushed after Natya. When he was halfway up the steps for the slide, he turned around, rushing down as she slid down the slide. He slapped her back. "You're it." Then ran like his life depended on it.

He chose the rope ladders and scrambled up them with no thought to how crazy he looked as he rushed away from the threat of being "it." His cheeks burned with how much he was smiling. He crawled through the closest yellow tunnel and looked out the plastic bubble window for any sight of Natya or Lara. His breathing was heavy, and his eyes darted over strangers. Then he spotted them on the side. Lara was at the top of a rock-climbing wall with Natya stopped halfway as they were talking. His eyes narrowed. They were conspiring against him.

He crawled forward through the winding tunnel, and when he reached the end, he could choose to go down or through one of four branching-off tubes. He went down. Halfway down was another set of tubes. He chose the one away from where Lara and Natya had been. If they were going to conspire, then he was going to hide, and they could have fun trying to find him.

He had no idea how much time had passed. They ran back and forth from each other, he continued to crawl through tunnels and watched them out the bubble windows. His stomach growled, echoing through the tunnel. Reluctantly he found the exit of a tunnel and took a slide down as he glanced around for them. He stood in the center of the room until the two of them made their way closer.

They stared at each other in a standoff, he didn't know which one was it and it looked like they were both wary, so it was hard to figure out.

"Truce?" Lara said. "Just until after we get some food?"

Roman glanced at Natya, whose gaze darted between them. "I'm hungry, so truce," he said.

"Fine. Truce."

It took another second before they moved and headed out of the playground area to the dining area after the girls grabbed their bags from a locker, where there were various tables, most of which were full. They found an empty four-person table and laid claim to it.

Nayta grabbed the menu. "They have pizza, nachos, walking tacos, burgers, and fries. You can add cheese or chili to the nachos or fries."

"But not to the pizza?" Roman asked.

Lara scrunched up her nose in disgust, but Natya laughed.

"Please order some chili pizza; I'm dying to see that conversation."

"Ugh don't." Lara shuddered. "I'm getting a burger." She stood up. "We have to order at the counter. What does the birthday boy want?"

"Walking taco."

"I'll take a cheese pizza, no chili though."

Lara headed off and Roman glanced at Natya who was smiling at him. "What?"

"I forgot we had another thing for you." She pulled out a small iridescent birthday hat from her bag. "Don't worry, we got them for us too." She handed one over and pulled one on her head.

He sighed and put it on; there was no point in fighting it.

"Good, now let me get a picture." She held up her phone. "Now, smile like this is the best day of your life." She tsked. "I guess that face is fine too."

After they ate and took another trip around the playground, they went back to the dining area where they brought out a cake, and he mentally thanked them that no one sang to him. When they stepped outside, the sun had already dipped far beyond the horizon.

"One drink," Lara said, lifting her index finger and pouting. "Just one."

"One," Natya repeated, batting her eyelashes.

He gave in. "Just one."

They got a ride back to campus so they could walk back to the dorms from the bar.

"Thank you," Roman said. Even if he was against the outing in the beginning, he needed it. He enjoyed it, it was the first time since he arrived that he actually liked being in Pennsylvania.

"No problem! Happy to be of service," she told him, with a wink. Before returning her attention to her phone with Natya leaning over as they murmured about swiping one way or another.

Lara wasn't Joss and he wouldn't think of replacing him, but she was a lifesaver thrown into the ocean when he was drowning. He hadn't found a way to connect with anyone on the team, but Lara was making it easy for him. In a way she was similar to Joss, pushing him to do things he didn't want to do but also choosing something that wasn't too out of the ordinary.

He knew Joss would be busy, but he had at least hoped for more effort. Even worse was his family. There wasn't much hope of them reaching out regularly, yet they hadn't even called or texted on his birthday.

The line at the bar moved quickly. The bar buzzed with conversation, and raucous laughter above the dance-pop music. Three bartenders were quickly shaking, filling, and taking orders.

The first drink was a shot, some kind of nipple, that was sweet and something he would continue to order if he didn't hate the name.

He protested against the second drink. One that tasted like hard candy. His protests went ignored, and he swallowed the shot.

The third and fourth were a blur of peppermint and chocolate.

If he had known they were going to drink so much so quickly, he would have eaten more. He held onto the table to remain stable. For the next round of shots, he made an excuse of going to the bathroom to avoid it. He took a sobering breath as he left the table that did nothing to stop the rush of alcohol streaming through his veins and causing his steps to wobble.

When he made it back, Lara grabbed his arm and tugged him toward the dance floor. Roman stumbled, the shorter woman adjusted her grip, not giving him time to refuse or pull away. The dance floor was suffocating. Too many people touched him. His body was floaty and his mind fuzzy. He couldn't breathe. There was no oxygen in the air. His vision blurred with unshed tears and sweat. He pushed and squeezed his way out of the dance floor away from the bar and into the cooling fresh air.

He sucked in deep lungfuls of air but it didn't clear his mind. The alcohol buzzed under his skin, numbing his entire body. His steps were unsteady; his body leaned against one of the buildings as he dragged his body forward. He stopped, fishing in his pocket for his phone until he realized it was in his other pocket. Finally freeing his phone, he called Joss. He needed a steady voice to get himself back to the dorm.

"Hello?" a cheerful voice answered.

Roman didn't respond, the world was tilting and his body swayed. Joss sounded strange.

"Roman?" another voice, lower this time, spoke up.

"What are you doing?" Roman's words slurred. He looked around, trying to remember which street he needed to turn down to get back to the road he was familiar with.

"Just messing around, what's up?"

"Oh sorry, you're busy."

"No, no. Not busy at all," the cheerful voice said.

The other voice was calm but worried. "Is there something wrong?"

Roman rubbed his face; his whole body was numb and tingly. "Can you talk to me until I get to my dorm?"

"Of course!"

Roman felt better knowing someone was on the phone, but it didn't help with his directions. All the streets looked the same with brick buildings and purple streetlights.

"I think I'm lost," he mumbled.

Just past the building he was leaning on, the street turned into residential homes, and he knew he hadn't passed them to get to the club.

"Can you share your location?"

"Uh, I think so." Roman sat against the last building on the block. His fingers were clumsy, but he could finally share his location.

"You're going to head back down the street, away from the houses," the calm voice said.

Roman followed their directions, with them only bickering twice. Roman was exhausted by the time he crawled into bed. He fell asleep to the sound of a stranger's voice. He would worry about sharing his location with a stranger later. At least he made it to his bed.

Roman woke up to the sun stabbing its rays into his eyes. His head pounded, and his mouth was dry. He checked his phone to see the time, but it was dead. Plugging it in, he grabbed his stuff to brush his teeth in the bathroom. Afterwards, he chugged all the water from his Capybaras-branded water bottle. Refilled it and drank half of it. He never wanted to drink alcohol again. The bed sank under his weight as he relaxed onto it; his limbs were heavy with the weight of a hangover. His phone vibrated with two texts. Ignoring those, he checked his call history first.

Joss Mobile 2:31 AM

Natya

> Send a selfie when you wake up.

Lara

> Are you okay??? Where did you go? You better not be kidnapped!! Rade???? Answer me?? Hello?? Oh shit, I never sent the text message. Can you hear me?? Hello?? Are you in the bathroom? Helllloo!

He sighed. Maybe it was Joss on the phone, maybe he and whoever he hooked up with had helped him.

He found Lara asleep in the common room. Grabbing a bottle of water and ibuprofen, he set them on the floor next to her hand that hung off of the couch.

Trudging back to his room, his mind drifted to his mom. All the frustration he had when he left was gone a long time ago. He hadn't talked to them for months. Maybe it was calling Joss last night, but he was feeling homesick. She hadn't called him on his birthday or texted him. It was strange. Maybe something had happened, and no one told him?

It rang several times, and when it got to her voicemail, he hung up. He waited a few hours, thinking it had been too early, but it reached the voicemail again. And again. He tried his dad, and it was the same thing. The last person in the world he was going to call was his sister; she probably wouldn't answer anyway.

He texted Joss, wondering if he would bring up the call last night. They were playing a game against each other soon and he missed his best friend.

Roman
Are you ready for the game next week?

Joss
Ugh hungover but fuck yes, I am.

Roman
Want to hang out after?

Joss
Duhh.

Roman
Dinner or what?

Joss
I'll call you and we can figure it out later. I need food and death.

Roman
Ok.

His mom might not have answered, but at least he would see Joss soon, and that was better than anything else.

8: Tee Tries Things Podcast

Tee: Hello my lovelies! This is Tee with Tee Tries Things. Welcome to this week's podcast. If you're new here, then hi there, and please don't judge me too harshly on my attempt to try things, which usually fail. But the fun is in the process. If you also want to *watch* me try things, head on over to my vlog. My podcast is basically just the sound from my vlog, with a few added tidbits.

   Tee: Today I am trying evobe. If you don't know anything about it, don't worry, I'm going to explain it as concisely as possible. There are two sides of the field, the row side, where a row of bunkers sit in front of the blocker boxes and the angled side, where blocks are angled in front of the blocker boxes. Now the most important thing in evobe, the players: a runner is a player on the field that gains points; either by hitting an opposing runner or hitting a target. One point for hitting other players, three, five, and ten for the targets depending on where you hit it, of course. Runners get ten arrows per period with five substitutions per game. A blocker does exactly what they're called: they block arrows inside of a blocker box. The team with the most points at the end of the game, wins.

Tee: I'm starting off as a runner today. I have my outfit on, long sleeves and leggings. The reason players cover their arms and legs, besides protection from the arrows, even though they're foam, is to be able to see the paint splatter. It's harder to see on sweaty skin. The arrows have tips that look like weird marshmallows. The tips have different colored paint inside for each team. I also have a helmet, when I first saw it, I thought it was a paintball helmet. They're very similar. It protects the entire head from arrows and paint splatters. I also have a wrist guard, arrows, and a bow. I've only done archery once before when I was seven at summer camp.

Tee: When shooting at other players, you can't aim for their heads, but the rest of the body is fair game. I didn't learn all the rules to play today we'll have to see if I break any rules unintentionally.

Tee: As you'll see in my vlog I didn't aim very well. It was hard to focus on aiming while also avoiding other players and getting hit. It was so much fun, though. I did climb a bunker and attempted to hit a target. I almost hit it, if I moved a little bit more I might have hit it. I swear! I was so close.

Tee: Then I tried the blocker position. Which was actually my favorite. Knocking the arrows away with the blocker pad was fun. I would do it again especially if I brought my friends and we did it together.

Tee: As for broken rules, I did pick up an arrow that I already shot. Which is a no-no. I also gave one of my teammates one of my arrows, they were a better shot than me, so I thought it was a good idea. Then I caught someone else's arrow, and unlike dodgeball, they don't get kicked out of the game, and also it was a point against me. No headshots, so yay me! That one is a penalty, and you are taken out of the game for like two or maybe three minutes. I don't remember. I think it's three.

Tee: Oh, and I did take my helmet off, which is against the rules, but I wasn't fully ready when the game started and just shoved my helmet on, but it's a whole helmet, like a motorcycle helmet. I can't just adjust my hair. You would think they would understand that.

Tee: If you guys are interested in trying evobe, I have all the information on my website. You can get a discount if you use my code, teetriesevobe30.

Tee: See you next time, lovelies.

9: DRAGONS

Roman gnawed on his lip, his leg bouncing as he flipped his phone in his hand. Joss had wished him luck and Roman returned the sentiment. His stomach churned with the idea of playing against Joss. Even when they scrimmaged in high school they were always on the same team.

"Alright." The coach clapped her hands. "Starting blockers: Park, Addams, and Ling. Substitutes in order: Walz and Morcilla. Starting Runners: Thongsuk, Gobbo, Tate, and Lamb. Substitutes in order: Singh and Wade."

Roman sat on the bench before the game started and stayed there when it ended. He didn't play. He still wasn't good enough. Maybe he never would be, maybe this was all a mistake, they had to be thinking that; everyone had to be thinking it. He wished he could be better, to do better, he just didn't know how. Nothing he did was working. He was trying, but he just couldn't reach everyone else's skill level.

Frustrated grunts echoed off each other in the locker room. His phone vibrated in the locker behind him, it took him several seconds to register the world around him. Mechanically, he turned around and opened the locker and answered Joss's call.

"Hey," Roman voice was low and a few people glanced at him, in different states of undress. He lowered his head, he hadn't even gotten a chance to play. To prove himself. To show Joss that he was doing well all by himself.

Joss's exuberant tone caused reality to materialize around him. "Hey! We're still meeting tonight, right?"

Roman hummed his agreement, he had a vague recollection of some kind of plan to meet up.

"We're going to get some food, you have to come to a club with us. I'll send you the address."

"Can't we just meet for dinner?" Roman asked. He didn't get an answer because Joss had already hung up. He didn't want to go to a club. The night would just turn into a drinking contest and they wouldn't have a chance to talk.

Natya banged her hand against the locker. "Let's meet up with the Dragons tonight! We may have lost the game, but we won't lose in drinking," she called out. There were a few protests that were quickly swayed with the offer of free shots.

Roman clicked the link that Joss sent over for the club, it was only two blocks from campus and a fifteen-minute walk from the dorm.

"We're getting dinner and we'll meet them later. So everyone head back to the dorms and get dressed. We have to look hot tonight."

Roman showered quickly, packed up his bag, and walked back to the dorms, it was only a ten-minute walk from the stadium that he turned into a twenty-minute walk. The crowds were on their way out, some were still cheerful, despite the loss.

By the time he got back to the dorm, the team was in the chaos of getting ready. Doors were wide open as people yelled out for opinions on outfits. He changed into a simple gray T-shirt and blue jeans with sneakers. A few people finished and hung out in the common room. He slipped out the door and into the cool night air. He wasn't avoiding them on purpose; he just wanted to enjoy the solitude before he was surrounded by drunken antics.

Roman relaxed on a bench he frequented between classes, waiting as time ticked down. The October night was mild, without a breeze. His legs shook. It had been five months since he had left Arizona and Joss. Dinner was preferable to meeting at a club, he thought Joss would agree. He swallowed his disappointment and attempted not to let it bother him.

The club was crowded when he made it through the doors. Maneuvering through floundering limbs and unsteady hands holding drinks full of alcohol was a nightmarish maze. He caught a glimpse of a few of the Dragons on his way in. Keira Barker stood out, with her long flowing red hair, her angular face was highlighted with glittering makeup in her dark green dress. Sumaiya Shea stood next to her in a black jumpsuit, that covered her arms and legs, with a deep red hijab that matched her bold lipstick.

He finally found the private room Joss directed him to from his messy text. The glass door opened when he pushed on it, there were two tables, and a long U booth with a space between each table to walk. *Glass walls and doors were a terrible idea in a building full of drunk people.*

The only free spot was next to Casper Graves near the door, with a wall of glass behind him. His wavy black hair nearly covered his eyes. His lips were slightly downturned. Roman gingerly sat next to him, waiting for a rejection that didn't come. Casper was reading on his phone, not noticing him. Roman relaxed and tugged out his own phone. It was old and slow and took a while to do anything. He didn't really have anything to do, but he was too awkward to just sit there and wait for Joss to arrive.

The group had decided something and all of them left. He looked up as TJ North passed by in a T-shirt and jeans, his face gave off a somber look, his light blue eyes were bright against his pale skin and dark hair. Roman glanced away, sneaking a look at Casper, then back at his phone.

Casper spoke lowly, his gaze never straying from his phone. "Some of them are getting shots for the group, the others are dancing."

His voice sounded familiar, but he couldn't place why.

"Oh, thanks." Roman set his phone face down on the table. Even if he tried to text Joss, he wouldn't necessarily get a text back and eventually he would come back to the room.

"I'm Casper." Casper half turned his body toward him; he wasn't nearly as intimidating as he expected. He was muscular but not bulging, his eyes calm and kind, his lips softening from a frown to something more neutral.

"Roman."

Casper's eyes flicked over him. "You're friends with Joss, right?"

"Yeah." *Friends with Joss not Joss's friend.* There wasn't a major distinction between the two phrases, except that whenever someone met him in high school, he had always heard the phrase Joss's *friend*. Roman always felt like an extension of Joss, instead of being his own person. By saying he was friends with Joss, it meant they saw him as a whole person. Someone who was close to Joss but not a part of Joss.

"I can move since they're gone now," Roman offered. The whole room had cleared out, allowing him to choose any seat.

"You don't have to. Demi was sitting there but he won't care."

"Oh, I didn't know." Roman started to stand up but was stopped by Casper's hand on his wrist.

Casper slightly shook his head, letting his wrist go. "Don't, I'll slide down and he can sit on your other side."

"Okay."

Casper slid down; Roman followed him. His mouth went dry and his mind went blank. All words escaped him. The door opened letting in a stream of loud upbeat music. Joss, Jax, Natya, Demi Knight, and TJ carried a few trays of fruity drinks and colorful shots. Relief flooded his body, he didn't have to try to think of something to talk about.

"Roman!" Joss set the tray on his table and ruffled Roman's hair. He looked the same as he always did, shaggy brown hair, eyes and smile that shone with excitement. His arm muscles looked larger in the gray henley.

"Take a shot with me." He tilted his head toward the clear shots on the tray. From Joss's demeanor, he didn't think this was his first drink of the night.

Casper reached out as well, the three of them each grabbing one. Joss winked at him before throwing the shot back into his mouth. Roman expected a bitter burn and was surprised with a sweet flavor with an apple aftertaste.

Joss looked him over. "You look good, not much of a tan still."

"Sorry, I don't want skin cancer," Roman muttered. "You look happy." There was something about Joss that was brighter, like he was finally able to be himself. Though Roman always thought he was himself.

"I'm pretty happy. College is fun." Joss grinned.

Roman believed Joss was having fun, maybe that was the difference, high school there were always rules, but in college, Joss was free to do whatever he wanted, and he was thriving, while Roman was wilting.

The door opened and Lara stepped in, she waved at Roman. She couldn't get any closer, blocked by Joss and Natya standing in the doorway.

"I'm Joss." Joss stood up straight, his eyes scanning Lara. Lara returned the look—a fresh gaze of interest.

"Lara," she said with a slight grin.

If Lara wanted Joss, Roman wasn't going to stop her. She hadn't shown any interest outside of platonic friendship with him, and Roman wasn't interested in anything romantic with her.

"Here, a shot." Joss handed one to Lara who took it and stared at Joss while she swallowed.

Roman shifted, suddenly uncomfortable. He glanced at Casper who was reading on his phone again, Casper glanced at him, then at Joss and Lara before he returned to his phone.

Roman clenched the bottom of his shirt in his hands. A hello and a shot didn't allow the bonding time he wanted with Joss, but he knew this was how Joss always was, and he had accepted it a long time ago. As soon as something shiny passed by, it diverted all of his attention. Eventually, it would lose its shine, but for now, it held all of Joss's focus.

Two more shots disappeared down Lara and Joss's throats and then with a wink and a grin they left the room with an explanation of *dancing*. Roman leaned back with a wistful smile. He turned and watched them through the throngs of people. Roman wouldn't call what they were doing dancing.

"Did your friend just steal your girlfriend?" Demi asked, causing Roman to jump. He had left the space next to him open for Demi, but he thought he would realize he was there first. Demi Knight had dirty blonde hair styled messy, dark brown eyes, and a large smile that showed off white teeth. What caught his attention were the black stud earrings in his earlobes.

"No, Lara and I are just teammates."

Roman noticed it was just the three of them left in the room, he wondered just how much he had missed in the few seconds he was watching the sweaty gyrating. Demi properly dropped into the seat next to him, sandwiching him into the booth with Casper.

"I was hoping to talk to Joss, but he's busy," Roman said.

"You still could." The three of them turned to glance as the gyrating devolved into making out. "Maybe not."

Roman laughed. "It's fine, I'll talk to him some other time."

"But it's annoying, right?"

"A little." Roman took another shot. Demi and Casper mirrored him. It wasn't Lara that annoyed him though; it was losing time with Joss.

"You have us to hang out with now," Demi stated, nudging their shoulders together.

"Thanks, you don't have to hang out with me, I'm used to being alone." The words slipped out like papers from an unorganized folder. He tinkered with the empty shot glass, finally he pulled his hands back into his lap. He was like the sibling that tagged along to a birthday party they weren't invited to.

Demi plopped his empty shot glass into Roman's empty one and then stacked it into Casper's. "That's depressing."

Roman's stomach rumbled in hunger, so he reached for another filled shot glass to stop it. His mouth filled with the flavor of apples, he swallowed, then stacked the empty shot glass into the others.

Casper and Demi reached for another glass, before it touched Casper's lips, he spoke. "Are you hungry?"

Roman nodded, slouching into the booth. "I don't think they sell food here."

Demi laughed. "Then let's leave. You don't want to be here anyway, right?"

Demi was right; he didn't want to be here. He would rather be in Joss's hotel room eating takeout and talking about all the new things in their life. He would even be happy if they could watch terrible TV and just exist together.

Roman sat up. Getting food with them was better than waiting for Joss to lose interest in Lara. "Okay, there's a bunch of food places just down the street."

"Alright, let's go to your favorite place then."

"Uh, I haven't actually been to any of them." Roman ignored their twin look of raised eyebrows. "But we can try one."

"Where do you usually eat?"

Roman fiddled with the shot glasses, twisting them back and forth. "Mostly the vending machines, they're on the way to my classes, besides it's really easy and never crowded."

Demi slid out of the booth. Roman followed him, then stepped to the side, letting Casper out. Casper led the way out of the room. Roman glanced at Joss and Lara, hoping one of them would see them leaving and stop them, but they never did; both were too interested in each other. Lara he understood, but Joss, it stung. Roman followed Casper's broad back through the crowd, one last look, just in case. Still nothing. He swallowed his disappointment; it wasn't like they would never see each other again, and he could always call or text him.

The lingering warmth of fall followed the sun, leaving a chilling wind. Roman shoved his hands in his pockets. The alcohol was like a thin blanket, keeping the worst of the chill off as they took the sidewalk back to campus.

"Sometimes I sit on this bench between classes." He pointed at the dark blue bench he sat at a few hours ago.

"It's a nice bench," Casper commented, then laughed.

Roman stared at him in shock. "You laughed. Joss said you never smile or laugh."

"Maybe I don't like him."

"Everyone likes him. Well, except this one teacher in high school. She really didn't like him."

"Why does everyone like him?" Casper asked.

Roman shrugged, pushing his bottom lip out. "I don't know." He pulled his hands out of his pocket to tick off his fingers. "He's friendly and everyone says he's good looking. He doesn't struggle to come up with conversation. And he—" He had sex, lots of sex, with a lot of people.

"I've only known you for like an hour and I already like you more than him," Demi said, throwing his arm over his shoulders.

It was warm being tucked into Demi's side. The three of them were all in T-shirts and he wondered if Demi was cold.

"You're just being nice," Roman said, ducking his head.

Casper snorted. "He's not lying. Joss is annoying. I'd much rather have you around."

Roman lifted his head to look at him in astonishment. "Joss is annoying?"

Joss was his best friend. He supposed it hadn't seemed like they were best friends since they started college. But he didn't think they had to talk all the time to remain best friends. It just sucked that the first time they had seen each other in months, he went off to be with someone else. He never thought Joss was annoying, maybe it was because they lived together.

"There's a vending machine." Roman pointed up ahead to a row of vending machines lit up like a lighthouse guiding ships. "I've been trying all of them; there are a few left I haven't tried yet."

Roman's steps quickened, forcing Demi to pick up his pace to keep up, explaining each machine and which ones he liked the most. Casper swiped his card and bought all of their food before Roman could even reach for his wallet.

They made their way back to his favorite bench. The scent of rich inviting broth rose with the clouds of steam. Fresh noodles and vegetables soaked in the broth. There were also chopsticks and sauce packets that came along with the bowls.

Demi and Roman had gotten two different ramens a beef and a chicken one, while Casper had chosen Japanese curry with white rice.

"So what is the deal with this?" Demi asked, lifting a few noodles on his chopsticks. He put them in his mouth, and Roman watched the noodles disappear past wet lips. "How is something from a vending machine so good?"

"I've watched them restock it every day, so everything is fresh."

"I see why you eat it so much."

"It's convenient and delicious." Roman grinned, taking a few bites of his own noodles.

"Can I try yours?" Casper asked, offering up his bowl.

"Of course." Roman traded with him and took a few bites before trading with Demi and then again with Casper to get his back.

It may have been the alcohol or the hot broth but it was as if he was in a warm bath, relaxed and happy.

Roman woke up feeling hot and hungry. He sat up to find a plate of buttered pancakes in front of him. He blinked several times, as if they were a mirage that might vanish.

"Breakfast," Demi said.

Casper's arms slipped away from Roman's waist. It was a tight fit for three men on a twin size bed. Casper and Demi weren't short or thin, they were well muscled and toned forcing them to press together so no one fell off the bed. Casper's arm had pulled back, but his legs were still tangled with Roman's. He vaguely remembered Casper murmuring in his ear about the wall being cold. Roman told him they could switch, but Casper said he would just move closer. There wasn't much closer otherwise they would have been on top of each other.

Demi then complained he was too close to the edge and was pressed into the shelf, and had shifted closer. Worried about bothering them and touching too much, Roman had slept as straight as possible, with his head tilted at a strange angle to avoid breathing on them. He tilted his head, wincing at the soreness. He wiped his face, in case he drooled. Then glanced at his shorts, sighing in relief. That would have been embarrassing. Worries piled up in his head like a grocery list.

"Mm tired," Casper groaned. His sleepy voice was low and slow. Roman turned towards him. His brown hair was tousled, and he slowly revealed his brown eyes.

Demi's voice pulled Roman back to him. "I didn't want to go crazy using other people's food, but there was a lot of flour and baking stuff."

Roman turned away and focused on Demi and the golden brown pancakes he was being given. He sat up, untangling from Casper. "I think someone made cookies a month ago, they came out looking like hockey pucks."

"Then I don't feel bad using it. Better we eat it, then let it go to waste."

Roman didn't understand how Demi had that kind of confidence. He lived there and never used anyone else's food. It didn't stop him from eating every pancake on the plate. His mom used to make him pancakes on his birthday with sprinkles in them, he had seen pictures that they had started from his first birthday with them. He supposed that all changed after his sister was born. There were only four photos of him and the special pancakes. The vending machine had become his source of food but to finally have a home cooked meal, it was nice. Then it was awkward as they all stared at each other. It was like a one-night stand without any of the usual activities.

Demi pointed a fork-speared pancake at him. "I'm glad you made it back that night, you kind of mumbled you made it and then the call cut off."

"What?" Roman asked. "What night?"

"You called Joss, and you were lost."

"Oh." So it hadn't been Joss and a stranger; it had been Casper and Demi. "Thank you. I drank a little too much that night."

"Hey, no worries, and if you want to call us in the future, you can. We're very good at directions. Well, I am." Demi waved the pancake around.

"You almost had him going the wrong way," Casper said.

Demi rolled his eyes. "Fine, Casper is good at directions."

Roman smiled. The blurry remnants of that call resurfaced. He didn't know what he would have done if they hadn't answered the phone. Maybe Joss would have helped him, or maybe Joss would have never answered.

After breakfast, Roman reluctantly walked them to the parking lot. He secretly hoped they could stay longer, but they had a flight to catch.

"You have to stay in touch, okay?" Demi said.

"Yeah."

Demi narrowed his eyes. "Don't forget that you promised." Demi pulled out his phone, showing him a video.

It was of the three of them, their hands entwined in a three-way pinkie promise. The camera shook, blurring their hands.

"You can't break the promise," Demi said, his words slightly slurring. *"I have proof."*

"I promise!" Roman yelled.

Roman pushed the phone toward Demi. "I remember."

Roman knew getting more alcohol was a bad idea. He didn't know what else he had promised or said, and he didn't want to find out. He waved as they got in the hired car and walked back inside. The last bits of warmth gave way to a numbing chill as the autumn air blew around him.

10: Halloween

After their loss, the team resumed morning practices, keeping Sundays free. Except for that night, and tomorrow morning for Halloween. Meaning they all agreed to practice on Sunday to make up for it. Roman didn't care for holidays, especially ones like Halloween. He preferred his Sunday off, but he was in the very low minority of one.

He used his morning runs to get to practice instead of relying on anyone else. He could have taken the bus, but he hadn't tried it yet and didn't want to risk getting on the wrong one and arriving late.

Roman still hated the dodger. Even if he was getting better at dodging the bars, he still didn't feel like he was improving at dodging arrows. The coaches shook their heads as they wrote down stats and info. Roman kept track and made sure he was shooting off enough arrows, but wasting arrows without hitting any targets or opponents made him look like an idiot. He tried to hit someone, but as soon as he released his arrow, the opponent moved. When he shot at the targets, the blockers knocked them away. His stats remained at the bottom of the runners. In his free time, he went to the archery range and shot at targets, but it wasn't the same as moving through the field and hitting humans.

He showered quickly after practice, ignoring the conversations about Halloween plans. He didn't have any plans, and he didn't plan on adding any to his agenda. The shower sprayed down cold water, washing away the sweat and disappointment. He still had classes to get to and didn't dawdle.

He had enough time to work on his art assignment in his dorm before heading to class. Roman crumpled the graphite-covered paper. He stared at the marks marring his skin, showing his effort but not his skill. He pulled out a fresh piece of paper and his phone, scrolling through Demi's photogram as a distraction and inspiration for his current portrait assignment. It was a treasure trove of selfies and pictures of Casper. There were some pictures of the other Dragons players.

In one photo, Demi wore an open black button-down shirt standing with Oakley Talkbot who had a shaved head and wore a dark blue blazer over a black bra and loose black satin shorts. She leaned her elbow on Alishba Shea's shoulder; her dyed blonde was up in two buns on her head. He wondered if she had done it to add a few inches to her height. Even with that attempt, she was still the shortest of the group, especially next to Meena Hays, whose legs looked disproportionately long in her short, skintight dress. It clashed with Ella Lin's more casual outfit of a T-shirt and ripped black jeans.

He didn't know what kind of party they were heading to, but the picture looked like they were in an emo rock band. They all looked good though, too good to ruin with his terrible sketching skills. He refused to glance at the pile of rejected attempts of disjointed proportions and unsightly scribbles. Lifting his phone, he took a selfie and forced himself to do a self-portrait. He would rather disfigure himself than someone else.

Demi

What are you doing?

Casper

Watching you act like an idiot.

Roman

Heading to class.

Demi

What class?

Roman

Drawing 101

Demi and Casper spent a lot of time together between living together and going to practice. They didn't have to text in the group chat to talk to each other. They could be sitting right next to each other for all he knew. Except he enjoyed being included in the conversation, even if he had nothing to add.

He got to class on time and set up the self-portrait he had started that morning. Roman jumped and slid his phone in pocket as a shadow cast over his easel. He turned around to his teacher, who was standing behind him and humming disapprovingly.

"Have you ever drawn a portrait before?" she asked.

He turned back to the easel and wanted to rip the sketch off and burn it. "No."

"What were you using as a guide?"

"A picture," he said hesitantly.

"Tell me your process."

"Well, I started up here with the hair and worked my way down here." He pointed to his left ear.

"So you did it in parts. Focusing on each individual part. It can work, but the with how your focusing, it's creating an imbalance."

"That's what I do with glass blowing when I have a big project. I usually have to figure out a base because I need to know how it will stand or if it will sit in something, and then I work on the rest." He stared at the portrait, seeing all of the flaws. Seeing the flaws didn't help him fix them.

"It's not a bad method, but I think it's what's causing your proportions to be off. Every artist has a way that works for them, everyone starts with the basics but eventually you find your style. We just need to find what works for you. It's a good attempt, remember to pay attention to the lesson."

Roman thought this teacher cared a bit too much, he didn't know why she was trying so hard to guide him, when this was just one class. He wasn't going to continue doing art. He also didn't understand why she made them draw first and then taught them how to draw.

"What's wrong?" she asked.

"Nothing." He pointed at his lackluster drawing. "Don't you think it's a waste?"

"What is a waste?"

He tilted his head to look at her. "Working with me?"

She smiled. "No. If I thought teaching a student was a waste of my time, I wouldn't be a teacher. You may never draw another thing after you leave this class, but while you are in it, I'm going to teach you."

"Ms. Timbal," someone called out.

"Keep working, I'll make my way back around. Then I will teach you all the Loomis Method."

Roman tightened his grip on his pencil. Taking a breath, he dove back into the drawing. It would never come out how he imagined but he had to try. Time slipped by, he stretched, stepping away from his easel as class ended and he started to clean up his materials.

He walked back to his dorm, some people were dressed up, most weren't. He paused in front of the dorm building, checked the scenery and looked again. It was his building, but it looked like a haunted construction site. Dummies in bloody construction outfits were strewn in front of the door. The entire doorway was covered in thick clear sheets of plastic with bloody handprints and smears coating them.

Roman stepped past the dummies and reached the door. A chilled hand wrapped against his ankle. He jumped away from the dummy sputtering swears and tripped toward the door as he heard low laughter. He rushed into the building, the walls had bloody construction signs and cobwebs streamed across the hallway.

"Hey Rade, Halloween party tonight," Lara called out from the common room where she was stacking purple solo cups on a black and orange decorated table.

"Okay." Heading to his room, he dropped his bag into his desk chair. When he was younger, he may have been excited, but the excitement faded quickly as he got older. In this case, he would stand out more without a costume. A box sat open with Dragons' gear Joss sent him. Roman pulled out the black sweats with Port Vista in white down the leg and a green Dragons' T-shirt. He finished up his homework while he waited for the festivities to commence.

When the noise and music were impossible to ignore, he opened his door and found the kitchen and hallway filled with costumed people. Each of their doors were covered in construction paper to look like jail cells with signs saying *keep out*. Roman stepped out of the room and weaved through party goers to reach the common room. He paused in the large doorway, people were crammed in, sitting on the chairs and the arms of the couches or pressed close together near the table of drinks.

He turned around and went back toward the kitchen, the counters were filled with various store-bought snacks. He chose an empty spot on the wall to munch on a few sandwich cookies.

Music started up in the common room, luring several groups of people that way. Roman remained rooted to his spot, Lara passed by him, stopped and sidled up to him. She lifted her phone, took a selfie and continued on her way. Lara was dressed as a killer cheerleader with fake blood splashed across the pink skirt and crop top and a knife tucked into her tall white socks.

Roman slipped across the hallway. He opened his door and paused as someone moaned.

He poked his head in, hoping it was a kitten, instead a grim reaper was eating out a blue fairy. He shut the door, then opened it again.

"Out, please get out," he said from behind the door.

He shut the door and waited. Less than a minute later, the door opened and the two headed for the bathroom. Roman opened his door, shut and locked it and then tore off all the bedding, shuddering as the mess hit the floor.

He sat in his desk chair, staring at the tangled sheets, blankets, and pillowcases. His face scrunched in disgust and attempted to not think about what kinds of fluids might be on it. Taking a picture of it, he sent the story to Joss.

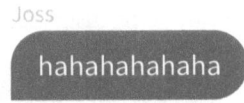

Roman didn't respond to Joss's message.

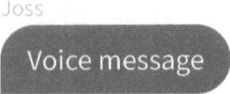

Roman glared at his phone where Joss's laughter rang through.

As a distraction he scrolled through Demi's social media. Neither he nor Caper were dressed up. Instead, the caption said: *I'm Casper and Casper is me.* Roman looked at the photo again but couldn't pick out how they were each other. Demi had a bright smile on his face, and Casper remained neutral. They were on a dark blue couch without any decorations in the background.

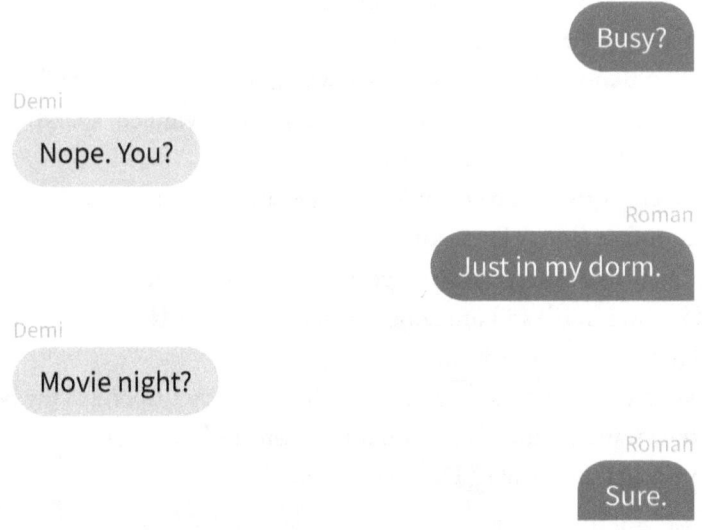

Roman accepted the movie invitation on his laptop and Casper and Demi appeared alongside another box with a black screen.

Roman grabbed his headphones. "Hey."

"Hey, mind if I choose the movie?" Demi asked. "I know it's Halloween, but I thought it would be fun if we watched a dumb comedy."

"I'm good with whatever." Any bit of annoyance at having strangers in his room, not being able to lay on his bed without being disgusted and Joss's laughter slipped away like a falling leaf.

While Demi chose a movie, Casper spoke up. "Are you wearing a Dragons shirt?"

"Oh." Roman looked down. "Yeah, I am. Joss sent me a whole box of stuff and since it's Halloween..." he trailed off. It felt stupid now, and he wished he had changed before starting the video chat.

"It looks good on you."

"Thanks." Roman tilted his head away, looking at the keyboard. His cheeks warmed under the compliment. "Um. Did you guys do anything for Halloween?"

Demi chuckled. "Nah, I baked some cookies, but that was about it."

Someone banged on his door, and Roman jumped. He ignored the duo laughter as he listened for someone to say something. It was quiet, and no one knocked again, so he put his headphones back on.

"Who was that?" Demi asked.

"I don't know, probably someone who got the wrong room."

The movie started up, and the conversation dwindled, sparking and fizzling with scenes in the movie.

Casper snorted. "They would never get away like that."

"It's movie logic," Demi said.

Roman also thought the escape was a little ridiculous.

"I know, but it's still unrealistic by movie standards."

"That's what makes it fun."

"No, it makes it annoying because I have already suspended my belief and they want me to believe—oh it was a dream."

"Now that is terrible," Demi complained.

"It's movie logic," Casper threw back.

"It's lazy logic. I can accept anything but a dream."

Roman laughed. The rest of the dorm noise rose several degrees. He tugged his headphones off to make sure there wasn't a fight or cops storming the place. Hearing nothing out of the ordinary, he turned the sound up on his computer and hoped it didn't bother them.

"Let me know if I need to mute my side," Roman said.

"Why, what's wrong?" Casper asked.

"It's noisy; I don't want it to bother you."

"I can't really hear it."

"Okay, good."

By the middle of the third movie, the noise died down. He slipped out of his room for a bathroom break and froze in the doorway at the mess. Solo cups, crumbs, decorations and strange stains littered the hallway. The bathroom was marginally better. Roman hesitated before grabbing a trash bag from the kitchen and filled it with trash. After filling the second bag, it was mostly vacuuming and stain removing left. He left the bags in the hallway near the kitchen, washed his hands and returned to his room to gather his bedding and throw it all in the empty washer. He grabbed his extra sheet and pillowcases and made up his bed again.

He unconnected his headphones from his laptop and laid on his side to finish the movie as it started up again.

"Are you going to fall asleep?" Demi teased.

"No," Roman murmured. His eyelids drifted closer together but didn't close, yet.

11: Dragons vs Foxes

November 5th

Period 1 | 20:00 | Dragons: 0 - Foxes: 0

Allen: This is bound to be an interesting game. The Dragons are playing with one substitute. Three of their players TJ North, Demi Knight, and Keira Barker are sitting out of this game due to a possible bar fight the other night.

Tamara: It's going to be a challenge for the Dragons. I don't think they can overcome it. Their captain and vice-captain aren't playing. Meena Hays will be the interim captain of this game.

Allen: It's definitely a game the Foxes' fans will want to record.

Tamara: The coin is flipped and the Foxes win it. They're taking the angled side.

Period 1 | 9:03 | Dragons: 7 - Foxes: 24

Allen: 9 minutes and some change left in the first period. It's been a brutal attack from the Foxes with no end in sight.

Tamara: The Dragons are trying to take as many points as they can but it's not enough.

Allen: Hutches aims at Talkbot's target. He releases and wait... Graves hits Hutches' arm. Hutches misses his shot, and Graves gains a point for the Dragons.

Tamara: That was one hell of a shot, the timing was perfect.

Allen: Graves is not slowing down, all of his shots are hitting runners aimed at targets forcing all of them to miss while he gains points.

Tamara: The only flaw to his plan is that he will run out of arrows and without a proper substitute he will have to sit out for 2 minutes before going back in. They have one substitute, who is a substitute, not only for the runners but also the blockers. If they don't use the substitute that's two minutes they are giving to the Foxes as an advantage, with the Dragons only having 3 runners on the field.

Allen: With 3 minutes to go and only 2 arrows left, he has a choice to make.

Tamara: It's made. 2 more points for the Dragons while Graves runs off the field to his bench in a two-minute waiting period. The reason we have these waiting periods is to reduce wasting arrows. It makes the players more mindful of their shots, especially with a limit of only 5 substitutes per game, but they can take as many waiting periods as they want. Very few teams would take that risk. No one wants the other team to have an advantage over them.

Allen: Barrera, Hays, and Shea are running around like children playing a game of tag. Lin, Shea, and Talkbot are struggling to block the arrows the Foxes are shooting at them.

Tamara: Barrera, Hays, and Sumaiya Shea all hit targets for the Dragons.

Allen: At least there was a plan for their madness. One minute to go and Graves is back in the game. I don't think he alone can change this game around.

Period 2 | 20:00 | Dragons: 16 - Foxes: 35

Tamara: It's the start of the second period. This may be a record-scoring game for the Foxes.

Allen: Galloway, Talkbot, and Alishba Shea are in the blocker's boxes. They have switched up their placements. Galloway is in the middle blocker box, with Talkbot on his left and A. Shea on his right. Time will tell if it will matter.

Tamara: The Foxes are starting off strong as they run for the targets. The Dragons aren't giving up. Hays and S. Shea are targeting the runners while Graves and Barrera rush for the targets.

Allen: The Dragons aren't giving up, we love to see a team fight from the bottom.

> Period 2 | 7:01 | Dragons: 25 - Foxes: 47

Tamara: Only 7 minutes left in the 2nd period the Foxes are ahead by nearly double the points.

Allen: This goes to show how important it is to have the right players on a team. Graves is a great player but he can't win alone. It feels like he's playing with a bunch of middle schoolers.

Tamara: The Dragons heavily rely on Knight to block shots and Barker to make target shots with Graves. Unless the blockers can pick up the slack that Knight and Barker have left behind, they aren't going to win tonight.

Allen: There is a dynamic to teams, and a core part of the Dragons team is gone. They should have forfeited this game instead of embarrassing themselves.

> Period 3 | 11:40 | Dragons: 31 - Foxes: 54

Tamara: With a little more than halfway through, the Foxes are ahead by 23 points.

Allen: If they got two bullseyes the Dragons would almost even the score making this an interesting game. I don't think we'll see those shots today.

Tamara: Graves has the ability, but the Foxes' blockers are focused today and aren't letting him through.

Allen: Graves' fourth arrow hits 3 points against Dell's target. Not enough to catch up as the Foxes continue to rain on the blockers.

Tamara: The Dragons aren't sitting around, but it's hard for runners to make up points that the blockers have already given away. Though it looks like Galloway has finally found his momentum, he hasn't let an arrow through this whole period, except it may be too late.

Allen: If Galloway had played like this from the beginning, the Foxes wouldn't have such an overwhelming lead. He has potential, as long as he can focus on the game in the earlier periods, he may surpass his seniors.

Allen: It's been a great game for the Foxes today. The Dragons did what they could.

Period 3 | 00:00 | Dragons: 45 - Foxes: 70

12: Notifications on

Roman sat on his bed, beads of water slipped down his neck, soaking his T-shirt. He absently dried his hair with his towel while he watched a new nature documentary on his computer. Dropping the towel, he rubbed at his shoulder, feeling a dull soreness.

Buzz buzz. He glanced at his phone.

Demi

> I'm bored, want to do a call?

Roman

> Sure, I'm not doing anything.

He paused the documentary as Demi's call came through.

"Hey." Demi's voice was low, like he was sleepy.

"Hi."

"How was your day?"

Roman shrugged. "Fine. What about yours?"

"Do you really want to hear about it? All the boring details or do you want me to give back a generic answer?"

"Give me all the details, tell me everything." He didn't need to watch a documentary when Demi could give one about himself.

"Alright, well it started off good," Demi said.

Roman got comfortable in bed as he listened and watched Demi talk about his day. Mundane things like what he had for lunch and his walk to classes. Meena said something stupid to the coach, so they got extra laps. It wasn't riveting information, but it was enjoyable. Roman admired

Demi and the way he became friends with everyone he met, a stranger he helped or someone he bought a coffee for because they left their wallet in their car. He was always cooking and doing things for the Dragons as the vice-captain.

The story hit a lull, and Roman asked, "What happened with the bar fight?"

"That was a misunderstanding. This guy grabbed Keira, I stepped in and TJ got caught up in it. We didn't actually fight, but the police were there and asked what happened. I guess someone took a picture or video, and that was it."

"You got suspended from the game for that?" Roman asked. They were forced to miss a game. Roman was missing games because he wasn't good enough.

"Yep." Demi popped the 'p' several times. "It doesn't really matter." His tone was flippant. "Tell me about your day."

Demi might not have cared about missing a game, but Roman did, he was supposed to be good. He got into his dream school; they thought he was worth something, and he was failing. He forced the thoughts away, not wanting to ruin the mood or bother Demi with his self-doubt. As Roman thought through his day, there wasn't anything interesting to share, but he could try.

Roman cleared his throat. "I woke up, ate an apple for breakfast and headed to class. Class was fine, but the teacher sucks. He's more of a read-the-book-and-learn type, which is a terrible way to be a teacher. If that was the qualification of being a college professor, then maybe I should apply next year."

Demi chuckled but didn't interrupt, and Roman continued. "Then I had practice, we didn't have to run extra laps. I grabbed some ramen for dinner and then took a shower, and now we're here."

Casper called him the next day. It was unexpected. He didn't know Casper or Demi wanted to talk to him, but it felt like he was being doused in honey and lemon juice. It was bittersweet, because he knew it would end. They wouldn't want to talk to him forever. Even Joss hadn't been able to keep up a consistent communication with him. He would have to enjoy it while it lasted, soaking in the honey until reality hit and all he would taste is lemon juice.

"Hey," Roman answered.

"Hey."

It was quiet for a few moments before Casper cleared his throat. "Demi said he called you yesterday. So it's only fair I call too."

Roman smiled. "We talked about our day."

"Mine was boring."

"Mine too."

Another few seconds of silence permeated the air. "Have you watched any new documentaries?" Casper asked.

Roman hummed. "A new one came out recently, and I just finished it this morning. They went in a different direction with it than I was thinking so it was pretty good."

Their conversation flowed like a shallow stream. Casper talked about his new book, and Roman listened as if he were the audiobook. It was nice just to talk about their interests. Roman pulled up the blanket, getting comfortable as he listened to Casper's low timbre.

They usually texted and only video called on Halloween to watch a movie. He thought their calls were an anomaly, something that wouldn't continue and would just fade away. That week, it all changed. Demi called him and then Casper and then they were both calling every day. Demi liked to talk about life, things that made up the world. Casper liked to talk about their passions, things that made them who they were.

Sometimes they called in the morning on the way to class, other times it was during dinner. The days slipped by in this manner. He texted them when practice ran late or when Lara asked him to study at the library. Joss's texts were even more sporadic. Sometimes they were short, and sometimes they were long; full paragraphs of texts about his classes or his teammates. Sometimes he complained about Casper and Demi, those were his favorite.

Joss

Ugh Demi loves to play house. Why doesn't he just leave evobe and go work at a restaurant?

Casper is so boring, if he was a spice he would be flour.

Demi is annoying. He made muffins for everyone but didn't give me one. Like it's a muffin not a car.

They won't even let me sit on the couch. I hate both of them.

Roman was sure that if Demi quit evobe, then Joss would claim he was the best blocker in evobe. It was a little thrilling to see Joss struggle to get along with Casper and Demi, while he got along with them so well.

He scrolled through his phone and stopped at an ad. It was something that Demi would enjoy, something he would drag Casper to. He hesitated for only a second before clicking on it and signing up. If it was good, then he would bring Demi and Casper to it.

That Sunday, Roman headed into the an unassuming office building following the instructions on the confirmation email. He joined the line and listened to the chatter.

"I'm really curious how this is going to play out," someone said in front of him. "Do we get to choose or are they choosing for us?"

"We'll find out in a second," their friend replied.

"I know, I'm just saying."

Roman signed in and put on his name tag. Then the entire group was taken to a large room. Several screens were placed around the room, one with a game board and one with the logo playing with neon lights lightening up the rest of the room.

"Hello and welcome!" a woman with curly red hair in a white suit greeted them. "Some games require a group, some are for duos, and some are solo. You will all be able to play every game; they take between five and twenty minutes. You set the scores and play until then. Then you can choose someone from your group to be a host or use the computer's host."

The whole setup was that they would play game show games, with no payout at the end. He thought Demi would have a lot of fun with it. Roman joined the first room, and it was a solo trivia challenge. He scored in the middle of the group, nothing impressive. Other games included figuring out phrases and the price of items. At the end of the hour, a sheet showed them their scores in each game and their ranking in the group they had joined. He carefully folded the sheet, with the number three at the top. He didn't win, but he did great out of a group of twenty-six.

13: Tornados

Good Luck! You got this.

Kick their ass!

Roman rolled back his shoulders. The dark pink uniform clung to his lean frame. He jogged in place as he waited for Jax to shoot his last arrow for them to switch. They were playing the Tornados today. He tried to ignore the nerves clinging to his body. His hands shook and his stomach squirmed. The lights were bright and cameras moved around. If he fucked up, then everyone would know. It would be shown on the internet a billion times; he would be a joke.

"Go," Jax said with a push to his shoulder.

Roman stumbled forward. He hadn't even noticed Jax. Steading himself, he moved forward, his eyes darting around for anyone in red. Sliding along the first bunker, he tugged an arrow from his quiver. It slipped, but he grabbed it before it hit the ground. Taking a breath, he nocked the arrow on his string and lifted his bow as an arrow hit his shoulder.

"Fuck," he muttered. He turned toward them, but they had already run off. He moved toward the center of the field. Because he wasn't as good on the bunkers, he stayed on the ground, his arrow poised for an enemy. There was a flash of red on a bunker diagonal from him, he lifted and tugged back the string and watched the arrow hit the thigh of an

75

opponent. He grinned even when he felt two arrows slap against him, one on his calf, the other to his back.

Lara shimmied her shoulders when she saw him. She dodged an arrow and disappeared behind a bunker. He shot at the opponent who attempted to hit Lara and missed.

The period finished, he walked off the field with four arrows left. After being handed a wipe, he scrubbed off the marks from where he had been hit. Lara grinned at him. Her helmet was off, and she had a light sheen of sweat on her face.

"I'll get the one on your back," she said, grabbing his shoulder.

"Thanks," he muttered.

"It wasn't terrible for your first game," she told him.

He didn't want to take his helmet off. Shame burned his cheeks. He messed up. "How do you know?"

She chuckled. "Well, you didn't fall, right?"

Roman tugged off his helmet, turning to her. Hiding in his helmet wouldn't change anything.

"Or did you?"

He shook his head. "I didn't fall."

"See, not terrible then." She lightly punched his shoulder.

He didn't agree with that, and from the looks of the coaches, they didn't think so either. He sat on the bench the rest of the game, and even though they won; it didn't feel like a victory.

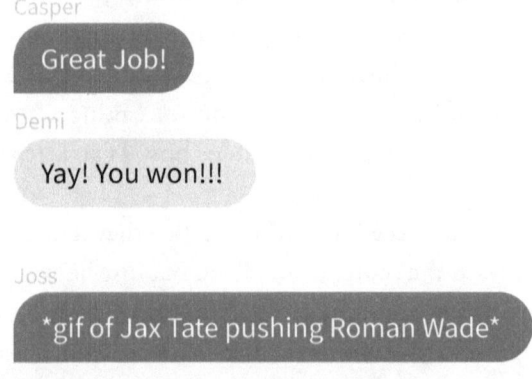

Roman put his bow away at the end of practice. It had been a couple of days since their game, but he didn't feel any better about it.

"Hey Wade," the assistant coach Fortin called out.

He waited for other names to be added, but it was only him. His bow slipped from his hand, and he scrambled to grab it before it landed. He smiled awkwardly at Fortin, who smiled kindly back.

Fortin waited as the team headed out before handing him a key and sheet of paper. "I want you to follow this extra regiment; it should help you catch up to the others. If you have questions, let me know. The captain said he'll help you if you need it."

"Thanks." Roman knew he had to do better. He was already staying a half an hour after most practices for target practice, and it still wasn't enough. He thought the Capybaras were a team he would thrive with. Each player had to bring their own strength to the team. Roman looked at the schedule. He had extra miles for running, more time in the Dodger or, as he liked to call it, "the bruise chamber," and extra time for target practice.

Groaning, he figured he could come back after dinner and get the extra hours in. It wouldn't leave him much time to do homework, though. Or he could get up earlier to add more time to his morning run. It was easier in the summer. Now that the season was in full swing, practices had gotten harder, and he had homework to finish and classes to attend. He pressed a thumb against the words on the paper. The bruise chamber didn't play to his strengths; he kept thinking too much about what the next step was instead of the one that was right in front of him. The chamber was supposed to help him with dodging; maybe he just needed to find something else to help him dodge.

His first full solo practice started that evening. Being alone on the practice field was an eerie feeling, like something was going to pop out from every dark corner. To combat the feeling he turned the skylight lights on creating a rainbow across the practice field. He tried to finish as quickly as he could; he didn't want to cancel his call with Casper and Demi.

Roman bounced on his toes, stepping left, then right. He added a few full jumps and ducks, his thighs and calves burned with the effort. Dropping to his heels, he noticed his phone vibrating on the bench in front of him. The screen lit up with a smiling Demi. He took a few slow breaths before answering.

"Hey," Roman answered.

"Working out?" Demi asked. Demi wore a loose black T-shirt, his hair tousled and damp.

Roman dug his toe into ground. "Yeah. I—uh kind of got extra work-out assignments. I guess I'm not doing as good as everyone else." He hated to admit it, especially to someone who excelled at the sport and someone he admired.

Demi hummed. "Is that what they said?"

Roman shrugged. "I'm the only one who has extra workouts." He looked around the room, if others had gotten assignments, then he wouldn't be there alone. And if he was doing great, then he wouldn't be having the extra workouts in the first place.

"Your issue isn't your playing or how fit you are. It's mental. You get a little lost on the field. Like when Jax pushed you, sometimes when the camera showed you, you looked like you paused or just stopped."

Roman groaned in frustration, tugging at his shirt. "I don't know how to fix it. I guess I didn't realize I spaced out so much."

"When you're on the field, what are you thinking about?"

He thought back to his last game. What had he been thinking about? Or more accurately what hadn't he been thinking about?

"Everything," he finally said.

Demi chuckled. "Easy. Next time don't think of anything."

"How?" Roman asked with an elongated ending.

Demi turned his head. "Hey, Casper, your brain is empty most of the time. How do you do it?"

"Fuck you," Casper said, taking the phone. "Learn how to breathe." Casper also looked as if he had just gotten out of the shower; water dripped down his neck from his hair.

"I know how to breathe." If that was his problem, then he would be dead and that might have made all of this a lot easier.

Casper shook his head, causing a few water droplets to scatter. "I don't mean actual breathing; learn how to relax on the field. People hold their breath if they're scared or stressed. You need to breathe or be on the field without overthinking it."

Roman sat on the ground, stretching his legs. "I don't know how to do that. I'm afraid of failing."

"It's not a test and it's not all on you. Trust your teammates to do their job. On a different note though, watch your shoulder and elbow when you're shooting. And don't dodge too quickly; that's why you keep getting hit. Your moves are obvious."

Roman took mental notes and then physical notes on his phone so he wouldn't forget anything. No one else told him exactly what he needed to do to fix his flaws. They just told him to work harder.

"Thank you," Roman told him, glancing at him again. They weren't teammates. Neither of them had to help him, but they did. He couldn't help but feel special; he tamped down the feeling. He wasn't special.

"For what?"

"Helping me."

"You know, my cousin used to get mad at me for pointing out his flaws. No one has ever thanked me before."

"It's really helpful." It was the most helpful advice he had gotten since arriving in Pennsylvania and it was from a "rival."

"You're welcome, Roman."

A lull in the conversation made Roman's mind drift, and a question come out before he could stop himself from asking. "Can I call you Cas?"

"You can call me anything you want."

Roman grinned. "Me too."

"You can call me whatever you want too," Demi called out. "I'm going to call you Roro. Isn't it cute? Don't ask me how long I've been thinking about it."

Roman set them on the bench as he listened to them bicker and talk while he finished his workout. Attempting not to blush at the nickname, but the heat filled his cheeks anyway. Luckily, he could play it off from the workout. He had never enjoyed a nickname more. He shoved his headphones in on the run home and listened to them like they were his favorite song. And didn't hang up until he made it back to his dorm and had to shower. He fell asleep with the duo lingering in his mind.

14: CRUSH

Roman kept his head bowed while he waited for class to start. The girls behind him were hard to ignore, even if he actively tried not to eavesdrop on their conversation.

The first girl's voice was on the verge of being nasally. "You haven't hooked up yet?"

The second one was light, almost airy sounding. "No, not everyone hooks up with the first person that likes them."

"But you like her."

"Yeah, and I want a relationship. Someone who checks their texts as soon as they come in. I want someone to be giddy to get a text or a phone call. Someone to care about what I like and buy me food or a small trinket because they think of me. I want—"

"Okay, I don't need a whole monologue, you want to date not hook up, message received."

"You're so unromantic."

The professor came in and the chatter died down. Roman tried to focus on the current discussion but the girls' conversation circled his mind. He thought about how excited and happy he was every time Casper and Demi texted or called him. And thought about all the new places and things he wanted to show them if they visited.

When he got back to the dorm, Roman read over his essay as he ate dinner. When he finished making a few tweaks he sent it in. After eating, he worked on his newest drawing for his art class. His head tilted back and forth, the proportion was wrong but he couldn't place where it was wrong. The girls' conversation crept into his mind like tendrils, taking hold and refusing to release him. He was never interested in hooking up with anyone, but he wasn't uninterested in a relationship. He didn't know how it would work, besides it being long distance, did people have relationships with three people? Would they be interested in something like that? Except people didn't just have two crushes, even if they did, he couldn't date two people. If he had to choose... Demi and his bright smile who always made him laugh, or Casper and his gentle smile who loved to talk about what Roman loved?

He threw himself on the bed. Maybe it was just a crush and it should stay that way, hoping for something more might just get him more hurt. He liked being around them and he could keep their friendship the same if it meant not losing them.

To preoccupy his mind, he started looking up different things to do in town and restaurants that were good for college students. In case they ever visited or if they decided to come during the summer. He ranked the restaurants based on his preference; he had to make sure the reviews lived up to his experience. His list grew from just a few to over ten places he wanted to check out.

The first restaurant on his list was busier than he expected. He chose a Tuesday night to avoid the crowd unfortunately it was one of the popular nights. He swallowed his nerves and followed the group in front of him to the hostess stand. The walls held old newspapers and wanted posters, it was in line with the restaurant's theme, a murder mystery. Each paper told the story of a murder and the wanted posters were suspects.

He was taken to a two-person table and handed a drink and food menu.

A waitress set a carafe of ice water on the table. "Welcome in, have you joined us before?" the waitress asked, he shook his head. "On the back of the menu is a mystery. You just fill out the grid with the given clues to find the answer. Each month we have a new mystery."

"Uh, okay."

"If you want to join our mystery month club, it's free to sign up with your email and you can get twenty percent off of your meal tonight and you also get a free drink and appetizer once a month. I'll give you some time to look at the menu."

It was a paper menu, on the front was the food and on the back was the mystery. Roman read through the story of a young man who was killed in his car. It told a story of a man cheating on his girlfriend and presented three suspects—the wife, the mistress, and the wife's best friend.

All plausible suspects with motives. He flipped it back over to the menu, each item was a play on "crime" words. *Blood splattered steak, Heist nachos, Alibi Alfredo, secret stash spuds, prison break pudding, black market brownies.* The drink menu had continued the theme. *Witness protection watermelon spritz, perjury punch, Bloody Mary mystery, crime scene cosmo, double cross daiquiri.*

He went back to the mystery after mentally deciding on the nachos. There was a grid with the suspects, weapons and locations and a box of clues. He just had to use the clues to fill in the grid and find the killer. He started with the obvious clues like the wife was in the garden at the time, but the murder happened in the garage. So it couldn't have been her. Some of the other clues took a bit of time to decipher, like figuring out if the mistress or the wife's best friend was lying. So he went through the rest of the clues, and the suspect facts and ticked off all the boxes until it all led to one conclusion.

The waitress came and went and he made sure to go over the clues before finding out it was the mistress that had done it.

Roman sat against his door, unable to sleep, and listened to Lara and Natya making cookies in the kitchen. It was after midnight when a metal bowl crashed to the floor. Pushing off of the ground to stand up, he tugged open his door, flour covered the floor. Lara and Natya were doubled over with laughter. Various ingredients were strewn across the counter.

"Rade!" Lara yelled out. "Help us make cookies."

Roman picked up the bowl and tried to help them. The problem was that they kept adding things into the bowl. As soon as he got a proper dough mixed together, he knew it was too much. He had to push their hands away to keep them from adding more mix ins. The cookies were filled to the brim with a mix of sprinkles, butterscotch chips, chocolate chips, toffee bits, and mini marshmallows. He quickly scooped out a dozen cookies onto a cookie sheet and shoved them into the heated oven. It was enough to distract the girls. He filled up another cookie sheet and put the rest of the dough in a ziplock bag, rolled it out flat and shoved it into the freezer. Roman rushed back and blocked the girls from grabbing the pan of finished cookies with their bare hands.

"Come on! I'm starving," Lara whined.

"Share the goods! Share the goods!" Natya chanted.

Roman pulled a few off of the hot sheet pan and onto a plate and handed over the crumbled cookies. The girls didn't mind and scurried off as soon as the plate was in their hands.

He stared at the flour caking the counter and floor, at the scattered mix-ins and sighed. He grabbed a broom from the cleaning closet, and a rag and started cleaning. When he finished, he washed his hands and took a cookie for himself, he took a bite and took a selfie with it and sent it to Casper and Demi. He was proud of the cookies he made and wanted to share it with them. Maybe he also wanted them to think of him. Before he could think too deeply about it, he crawled into bed.

The next morning he was presented with a bag of assorted breakfast treats from Lara and Natya.

"We owe you for helping us last night," Lara said, lifting the bag higher.

He took the offered bag. "Thanks and you're welcome."

Lara gestured with her hands. "They are so good. I thought it was because I was drunk, but I had one for breakfast and it's just ugh." She groaned.

Nayta said a quick thank you and headed off, leaving Lara at his door.

"I tried to add more dough, so it wasn't just mix-ins," he explained.

"And for that, I owe you my loyalty." Lara bowed with an arm across her chest. She quickly straightened. "But seriously, thank you. For cleaning and fixing the cookies. Who knows what kind of disaster we all would have woken up to."

"Probably the fire department breaking down the door."

Lara laughed. "You're probably right. You saved everyone. Now everyone owes you a life debt."

"Are you into fantasy?"

Her neck stretched out, her eyebrows raised. "Uh, yeah. A lot. I love fantasy everything." Her arms waved out in emphasis.

He fidgeted with the bag in his hands. "Casper gave me a list of book recommendations. I can share it with you."

"Casper as in Casper Graves?"

"Yeah." He didn't know anyone else named Casper.

"He likes fantasy books?" She leaned closer, her eyes narrowed in suspicion.

"Yeah?"

"I thought he just read business books."

Roman frowned. "I don't think he does, he's not taking any business classes."

"Casper Graves is a fantasy nerd. I need to write this in my journal," she muttered to herself as she went back to her room.

Roman shut his door, setting the food on his desk he sent a picture of his breakfast to Casper, Demi, and Joss. He wanted to show off, just a little bit.

Roman

Lara and Natya brought me breakfast.

Attachment

Demi

I'll make you something better than that.

Casper

Looks good.

Joss

I'm starving. TJ made some spinach egg thing, it's wet and gross.

Roman snorted. He wondered if he was staying more with TJ since he had a dorm to himself and Joss wasn't getting along with Casper and Demi. After breakfast he hung out in the living room, sketching. Some of the other team members filtered in, lounging on the couch.

"Who made the cookies?" Jax asked. "They're actually good, so what's wrong with them? Are they poisoned? If I get sick—"

"Oh shut up, there's nothing wrong with them. Why would you eat one if you're going to complain about it?" Lara asked, coming into the room. "Also, Roman made them."

"Oh, then I'm getting another one."

"He's so dramatic." Lara sighed, throwing herself into an empty chair.

Roman thought back to ten minutes ago when she was bowing and talking about life debts, that was more dramatic than worrying about food poisoning.

Later that night, Roman lay in bed, scrolling through Casper's photogram, it didn't take long. Most of his posts were for the team, promos and stuff. Demi's was an eclectic collage of his life since starting college.

He didn't know if he created one for college or if he deleted everything before his first day. Demi's first post was a selfie of himself standing in his empty dorm, it was taken in the living room, he could see the hall leading to more rooms and the edge of a kitchen. The caption said *"First day! Hope my roomies brought a couch."* He scrolled on, Demi showed what he ate for lunch or dinner. He had pictures from going out, glitter on his face shined in the club's lighting, it rivaled his open-mouthed smile, his eyes crinkled in delight.

As Roman scrolled through, he noticed a pattern with Demi's clothes, in the sense that there wasn't one. Casper wore nice name brand clothes, comfy but expensive. If Roman took a photo of his own clothes every day, the only difference would be brand and color. If the brand was covered and the pictures were in black and white, he would look like a cartoon character that never changed their clothes.

Demi wore different styles every day of the week. A leather jacket and tight jeans one day. The next he wore a soft looking cardigan and chinos. When he went to the club sometimes it looked as if he wore paint as clothes. Other times he would be in a T-shirt and jeans. He continuously took photos with the other Dragons, the only people he didn't see much of was Ella Lin, just the one photo with her, and TJ North, who wasn't in any of the photos. Otherwise, Keira was in them more than anyone else, even more than Casper.

Roman went through the photos trying to find his favorite look, but everything looked good on Demi. Nothing ever looked out of place. He paused on Demi in a loose crop top and short jean shorts. It was a mirror photo, he could see Casper glancing over to the camera in boredom.

The caption was: *just a gym bro being a gym bro, y'know?;) I might cut the shorts shorter.*

Roman tapped his phone, lighting it back up, he watched a pink heart appear on the photo. He stared at the fading heart in horror. The photo was taken over eight months ago and hundreds of photos deep on Demi's photogram.

Roman banged his head on his bed, he should have made a private photogram. He thought he may use it for his promo stuff if he needed to. He didn't have any followers because he didn't tell anyone about it. His body froze as a notification came in.

DemiKnightingreenarmour started following you.

A text from Demi came in with a photo attachment.

It was the photo he just liked on Demi's profile except Casper was smiling in this one as Demi posed like a magical girl.

Demi

> **Attachment**

> **;) thought you might enjoy this.**

Roman shoved his face into his pillow, muffling his groan. He picked his head up and shivered again at the thought of having to respond. He had to respond. It would be even more awkward if he didn't.

Roman

> Thanks!

Roman wanted to slam his head into the wall. He was an idiot.

15: Thanksgiving

Roman typed up his essay while his phone was propped up against the screen where Casper and Demi discussed a new TV show. They had a differing opinion on the main character, Demi liked them, he thought they added a dramatic flair and Casper didn't, he thought it was a failed attempt at adding humor to dark material.

"Hey Roro, what are you doing for Thanksgiving?" Demi asked.

It took Roman a second to register he was being talked to and another second to take in the words. He hummed as he finished his sentence before responding. "Nothing."

"Wanna come here?"

Roman looked up to see his face, it didn't look like he was joking. "Really?"

Demi nodded with a smile. "Yeah, we're not doing anything, but we could. Maybe remix some traditions or just order a pizza."

Casper spoke up before Roman could answer. "I'll buy your ticket and you can stay in the dorm with us."

"You don't have to do that," Roman said. He would pay whatever he had to.

"I want to, think of it as a late birthday present if it makes you feel better," Casper said. It did make him feel better. "It's settled. I'll buy the tickets."

He grinned. It was better to let them do what they wanted because in the end, he was getting something he wanted.

> **Roman**
> I'm going to be in Port Vista for the break.

> **Joss**
> Yes! You can stay in my dorm instead of a hotel. I never sleep there anyway ;)

> **Roman**
> Thanks!

He was already planning on staying in his dorm, even if it wasn't necessarily in Joss's room. But a bed was always better than a couch. He wondered if it was a good or bad thing that Joss, Casper, and Demi couldn't get along. Joss was his best friend, but he couldn't stand the idea of them getting too close to each other.

According to the pilot, Georgia greeted him with a cloudy sky and light wind, creating the perfect sweatshirt weather.

> **Roman**
> Just landed.

> **Demi**
> We parked and are waiting near the exit.

> **Roman**
> See you soon.

Roman hesitated inside the airport. People passed by him, some reunited with loved ones, others left by themselves. *What if they were just being nice? What if they didn't really want him to visit?* He twisted his shirt with his fingers, his duffle bag heavy on his shoulder.

> **Demi**
> Excited to see you!

Roman took a step forward then another, until he stepped outside. Cars honked and traffic was being directed to keep moving. He scanned the cars until he saw Demi hanging out of the driver's side waving his arms in the air.

When he got closer, Demi jumped out of the car and wrapped his arms around him in a tight hug. Casper moved slower, pushing the door open and grabbing his bag from his shoulder, throwing it in the trunk.

The fear and anxiety slipped away, replaced by a racing heart and a fluttering stomach. Demi let go, and Casper smiled at him, patting his back a few times before getting back in the car.

Demi drove around Port Vista showing off the meager sights it held. The tour was short and ended at the dorm. He liked the calm small-town atmosphere or maybe he just liked a few certain people living there. It was so much better being with them in person than just seeing them through a screen. He could reach out and touch them; they weren't going to disappear with the press of a button.

"This is the dorm building, I know it's a sight to behold." Demi turned around in the front seat after he parked. "Are you hungry? I was thinking we could go shopping later."

"I'm not too hungry yet, I can wait till we go shopping."

The newer two-story building stood out among the older six-story buildings like a young child among older brothers.

Demi opened his dorm door, and Roman followed him in. "Joss said you were going to stay in his dorm. He actually got more annoying when he found out you were coming."

"Really?"

"Really really."

A sense of satisfaction and warmth filled his body. He and Joss hadn't kept in touch as much as he had hoped they would before they left for college. His busy schedule and talking to Casper and Demi masked the loss. He was excited to finally spend time with Joss and learn why his updates were sporadic. A few texts didn't equate to the hours they used to spend together.

The reason clearly presented itself in the form of TJ North. He knew instantly that TJ was more than a friend or fuck buddy. Joss was holding his hand as he pulled him down the hallway toward him. He had never seen Joss hold anyone's hand before.

Joss grinned widely, waving with his free hand. "Roman! You made it. I could have picked you up, you know." Joss had gotten a haircut, and he looked taller.

"Did you get a car?" Roman asked, wondering if it was something new that he missed.

"I could have borrowed Casper's," Joss joked.

"No, you couldn't," Casper responded.

Joss ignored him and launched himself at Roman into a tight hug. "When did you become friends with these assholes?" Joss let go but didn't step away. He took a second to breathe in that familiar smoky orange scent. He hadn't realized how much he missed it or how glad he was that he hadn't changed it since starting college.

Roman tilted his head, he thought Joss knew? *Had he not told Joss about it?* "We met at the club when you were in Harmony."

"Oh. I barely remember that night. TJ ended up carrying me back to the hotel."

"Better him than a stranger," he said, his thoughts straying to Lara and snapping back to Joss.

Joss laughed. "What's the plan then? Are you staying in my dorm?"

"Yeah, where are you going to stay?"

"I'll be at TJ's, he has a dorm to himself."

Roman had seen TJ, but they had never officially met. "Okay, I'm Roman by the way." Roman titled his head to properly see TJ around Joss.

"TJ." TJ leaned forward but didn't put his hand out to shake so Roman didn't either, he just nodded. TJ's dark hair made his light blue eyes and light freckles scattered across his straight nose pop.

Joss patted his shoulder. "We should go out or get some take out."

"We were thinking of going shopping," Demi said. Moving closer, Joss shifted back to his place next to TJ, and Demi and Casper stood with Roman in between them.

"That will take forever, let's just go eat out," Joss said.

Demi shrugged. "Whatever works, we can go shopping tomorrow or something." Demi nudged their shoulders together.

"I'm good with anything," Roman responded.

They stood in a strange standoff until Joss spoke up. "We can all drive together."

"I'll drive," Demi called out quickly.

Roman sat in the back with Joss in between him and TJ.

"So how's Pennsylvania?" Joss asked.

Roman sighed, wishing he could say he loved it. Wishing he could look as happy as Joss did.

"It's okay."

"What's wrong?"

"Nothing, it's just not what I thought it was." Roman picked at his jeans. He should have tried harder to get into Port Vista. He should have wanted it just as much as Joss. If he had, maybe he would be happier. Or maybe he would be the one getting annoyed at Demi or Casper over something stupid. Maybe he would be the one crashing at TJ's because he didn't want to hear Casper and Demi bickering, or Demi clanging pans in the morning. He liked all of those things, he liked listening to Casper and Demi bicker. He liked watching Demi cook in the morning, even if it was across a screen. He liked listening to Casper complain about how a movie was illogical. Everything Joss hated was everything he wanted.

The restaurant Joss chose was low key and nearly empty.

"Usually it's packed in here," Joss told him. "They have pretty good burgers."

Roman hummed as he looked around at the decor, it just looked like a burger place, nothing outstanding.

They slid into a round table booth, Roman sat in the middle between Joss and Demi with TJ and Casper on the outsides.

He expected awkward and strained conversation instead it flowed like a well-fed river. They talked about evobe and other players, video games and TV shows. It felt natural and the conversation never went stagnant. He was glad no one brought up his game of shame. He still constantly saw the gif of Jax pushing him.

He started to regret wishing he was rejected from Port Vista. He could have had this the whole time. The conversation died down when the food arrived and Roman bit into the large jalapeño popper burger.

They ended the night with a movie in their dorm and for the first time in months, pressed in between Casper and Demi with a soft blanket across his legs, he was utterly comfortable.

Roman followed Casper and Demi into the building they called The Oven. It was an indoor practice field, less nice than the Capybaras' field. He could tell it was converted into an evobe field instead of being built as an evobe field. Roman slowly lifted his borrowed bow, the arrow aimed at a geared-up Demi and the target behind him.

"Are you sure this is how you wanna spend your free time?" Demi yelled.

"We don't have to do this all day. I just want some pointers," Roman responded with a measured breath out.

Casper placed a hand on his shoulder. "Too tense."

Roman relaxed his shoulder and his bow dipped. His shoulder had been bugging him the last few weeks, and it gave a slight twinge that he ignored.

Casper tapped his wrist up. "You can relax without losing your form. If you're too stiff you might strain a muscle."

Casper touched him nearly everywhere, making comments and sometimes fixing his shirt.

"I think he can shoot now," Demi called out.

Casper huffed a laugh near his ear, making it itchy. His mind went blank and his fingers trembled. He remained in position, refusing to move even an inch, and when Casper said to go, he let go of his arrow. Demi batted the arrow away effortlessly.

Casper cleared his throat. "Let's do it a few times. Demi, move out of the way," Casper yelled. It was the loudest he had ever heard Casper speak. "I want to see how your aim is," Casper told him.

Demi dropped his arm pad and tugged off his helmet. "I'll help position Roman," he said, then skipped toward them. Roman smiled at the silliness. He wished he could transfer right then, just leave the Capybaras and play for the Dragons. Except life didn't work like that.

Now, both of them continued to adjust his body, sometimes contradicting each other.

"Can I shoot now?" Roman complained. He wanted their help, but it was starting to feel like groping. Not that he really minded, but he was trying to focus, and he really did want their help. Besides, if they touched him too much, he might end up with an embarrassing problem.

Their hands disappeared. "All good now," Demi said, patting his shoulder.

Roman let out a breath. It was easier to concentrate when they weren't touching him. He focused on the target and let go. It slammed into the bullseye, leaving a green splatter behind.

"Your aim is good," Casper murmured. "What are you thinking about when a blocker is there?"

"How to get past them."

"That's it?"

"Yeah." Roman stared at the splatter mark. "I mean, I get worried if I can get past them or not. If I can get any points or if I'm wasting an arrow by trying."

Silence followed his answer. He glanced back at them.

"Shoot again," Casper said.

Roman grabbed an arrow, nocked it, lined up the target and let go. It splattered against the bullseye.

"You have some minor issues with your form. Your biggest issue is your anxiety. When you shoot at a target, you're not as tense. When Demi is in front of you, you tense up," Casper explained.

Demi spoke up, continuing with Casper's line of thought. "You calculate your shot too much, even if you don't think you'll hit the target you should take the shot. As a blocker, I'm constantly checking for runners, if I see one taking a shot from the left, I'm going to guard against it, but I might miss you taking a shot from the right. Your team doesn't coordinate shots enough, like everyone is out there on a one-man team."

Roman nodded, because that's what they were. A team of individuals. Though they ran coordinated drills, the focus was on individual strength.

"Can we do a few more shots? Then we can get some food or whatever you guys want to do."

"Against me or without me?" Demi asked.

"Against." Maybe if he could get past Demi, he could get past anyone. Even if it was an impossible task. He wanted to try.

Demi picked up his gear, and Roman took a few steps back. Casper stood to the side to watch. Roman stopped being serious and decided to have fun, he wouldn't get the chance to play against them very often and there was no way he was going to beat Demi. Once he let go of caring if he hit the target or not, he started having fun teasing Demi and shooting at his feet or his elbow and shoulders.

"Your aim is really good," Demi told him.

"Thanks," Roman said, as he tugged off his helmet. He ran a hand through his damp hair. "I should probably shower before we get food."

"We can just grab something on the way back."

Roman wasn't picky, he shrugged and packed away the borrowed bow.

Later that evening, the group of five sat in Demi and Casper's living room discussing Thanksgiving plans.

"As long as my brother can come, I don't care what happens," TJ said. Roman liked his voice. He wondered if he was ever interested in doing audio work. It was soothing and rich.

"He can come," Demi said. "Is there anything he doesn't like? Or something he would really want to eat?"

Roman liked Demi's voice too. He didn't mean to constantly compare people, it felt inevitable and uncontrollable. The differences between Casper and Demi were immeasurable, but he liked them equally. In certain moments, he liked one more than the other, but if he put everything on a scale, it would end up with the same weight.

TJ stared at him without answering, long enough for everyone to look over. "No allergies and he doesn't like onions, tomatoes, or lima beans. I'm sure he would like any kind of dessert."

"How old is he?"

"Seven."

"Okay, I'll get ice cream, just in case he doesn't like pumpkin pie." Demi added it to the list and TJ shifted like he was uncomfortable or proud, maybe something in-between.

Roman was still trying to figure TJ out. He was in a relationship with Joss, but Joss hadn't told him about it, which was weird. Joss was always open about his "relationships," but that was exactly what made TJ different. TJ was like a butter knife, he gave the illusion that he was sharp but he wasn't at all.

He had to be the reason Joss's communication had been few and far between. Joss never shied away from telling him every detail of his sex life, but since going to college he had only gotten one or two of those texts and then it was about the team, replying to his texts or Joss's mom saying hi. A part of him was happy for Joss, but another part felt left out, left behind, abandoned. *Why did he have to hide his relationship? What made TJ so special? Would everyone eventually leave him?*

"Any other suggestions?" Demi asked, waving his phone with the list lit up.

Roman shook his head. Forcing his thoughts away, forcing his feelings down. He clenched his hands then released them. *He was fine. He was fine. He was fine.*

"Who's going with me?" Demi asked. "It will either be a mad house or completely empty."

"I'll go," Roman offered. He needed a distraction, something to do.

Casper and TJ shook their heads.

"I'll go too," Joss added.

Roman hopped up, followed by Joss and Demi. The store wasn't far from the dorm building. Joss chattered about inconsequential things making the ride even shorter. When they parked and Demi got out and shut the door, Roman spun around in the front passenger seat.

"Why aren't you saying anything about TJ?" He had to ask. He needed to know.

Joss paused his hand from continuing to open the door. "He's a private person."

"You never told me you were dating him."

Joss's eyes widened then softened. "Dating, I guess we are... Dating." Joss pushed open the door, hesitating to get out. "I'm dating TJ," Joss told him.

Roman forced a smile. "I'm happy for you. He seems nice." He *was* happy for him, he just wished it didn't feel like a rift in their relationship, an iceberg threatening to tear them apart.

Joss laughed. "Nice?"

"I mean not nice in a *nice* way, but nice in a *he seems to like you and is happy with you* kind of way?" Roman had no idea what he meant, words were just a jumble of letters together.

Joss grinned, ducked his head and fully pushed open the door. Roman followed him out and joined Demi at the trunk.

"You good?" Demi asked.

Roman nodded. He was good even as envy and happiness mashed together, making it difficult to parse through. Joss was happy and in the end, that's what mattered.

The store was packed and the shelves were barren of the usual Thanksgiving ingredients. They were skipping some of the staple choices. Instead of turkey they were doing steak, instead of sweet potatoes they were doing french fries. They were doing what fit them and was still available. Roman was just happy to have something more than the suffocating silence of his own dorm room. There was a vibrancy and vivacious energy in Port Vista.

Joss bumped shoulders with him as he threw a bag of chips into the cart. "Are you going home for Christmas?"

Roman held onto the half-full cart, his grip tightening.

"No." They hadn't called or texted or even emailed him. They never answered his calls or texts. He was sure the last thing they wanted was for him to show up for Christmas.

Demi added a bag of potatoes to the cart, effectively ending the conversation.

"I think we're almost done," Demi said, scrolling through the list. "We just need milk and I think we're good to go."

"How do we want to split it up to pay for it?" Roman asked.

"I can take my snacks and a third of the rest," Joss offered.

Demi nodded. "Alright let's do that. Joss will pay for his snacks and a third of the groceries and I'll cover Roman's."

"Really?" Roman asked. It wasn't like he didn't have money, he could afford a third of the groceries. He had been careful with his money, barely spending any of it.

"Woah, that's not fair."

Demi snorted, looking at Joss. "As long as it gets paid, who cares who pays for who?"

Joss pointed at himself. "Because I'm one of the people paying."

"And? I'm not asking you for more than you were initially paying for."

"But—"

Demi cut him off. "But nothing, he paid to fly here. The least you could do is pay for some food."

Roman didn't want to get into the middle of their argument, though he didn't pay for his plane ticket, Casper did and Demi knew that.

"When you put it like that," Joss grumbled.

Joss had always been strict about money. He never allowed Roman to pay for him and he never paid for Roman. They always split everything in half.

Demi shook his head, tugging the cart. "I didn't realize you were so stingy with money."

"I don't like owing people, and I don't want anyone owing me anything. Everyone should just pay their share and that's it. How is that hard to comprehend?"

"I don't have any problem comprehending your point of view, I just don't agree with it."

"Whatever, let's go."

Joss sped up leading the way to the checkout counters. Roman glanced at Demi, who winked at him and grinned. Roman shook his head, with a roll of his eyes he followed Joss. Demi's quiet chuckle trailed behind him.

Roman stepped away from the cacophony of chatter and dishes clanking. He went into Joss's room, shutting the door to muffle the sounds. The dorm room didn't hold much personality, it was obvious Joss didn't spend much time there.

He called his mom and dad, but neither of them answered. Then he sent them a happy Thanksgiving text, but they didn't reply. He didn't know why he expected them to care about him. They were ready to ship all of his things out the door as soon as he left for college.

Roman relaxed on the bed, the door swung open and shut again as Joss joined him. All thoughts about his parents pushed to the side.

"You never told me you were so close with Knight and Ghost."

Roman wondered if now was the time he should share the status of his own strange relationship. But he didn't know what to say or how to describe it or even if there was anything to tell.

Roman shrugged. "We haven't kept in touch as much as I thought we would."

Joss joined him on the bed, nudging their knees together. "I didn't realize how fast time would go by."

"It's been slow for me."

"Do you like Pennsylvania? You said a bit about it yesterday."

"I like some of it, but I like it here more."

"I was right that it would have been better if we got in together."

But Roman didn't get accepted to Port Vista. Instead, Samia Barrera joined the team. She was good too, better than he was. The Dragons were having their best season since evobe's inception. He expected Joss to go after her, with her dark hair and brown eyes, she was pretty in a natural way that Joss always seemed to gravitate toward. Everything he thought would happen in college, ended up being completely different.

Roman circled back to the beginning of their conversation. "Did you say ghost?"

"What?"

"When you said Casper and Demi's names, did you say ghost?"

"Oh, yeah, that's his nickname."

"Really?"

Joss shrugged. "That's what everyone else on the team calls him, they call Knight, Demon sometimes. I don't think anyone calls him Ghost to his face but he's pretty standoffish. Knight is the only one that talks to him, but it's more like at him cause Ghost never responds, that's probably how he got the nickname."

Roman sighed at Joss's description. That wasn't how Casper was at all. Maybe Joss saw him differently because they didn't like each other.

"Why is Demi's nickname Demon?"

"Because he sold his soul to be unnaturally good at blocking arrows."

Roman stared at Joss. Not sure if he was joking or not or if that was really a theory that was going around.

"I'm serious. There's a bunch of forums called *Demi the Demon* with theories on how he's so good. It's unnatural. Plus, he literally tells us when we mess up in games. How can he see us on the other side of the field?"

"The screens?" That was the only explanation Roman could think of.

"Okay, so he's watching the screens, the rest of the field and people shooting at him while blocking all of the arrows?"

Roman's eyebrows creased with a frown marring his face. That would be really hard. Demi's ability to focus must be insane.

Joss continued talking, "Except for Ghost, who sometimes scores against him. Anyway, the whole nickname thing, I think maybe everyone else is treated like ghosts to him so it's payback?"

The idea of the team using a nickname as payback made him uncomfortable, but it wasn't his team and it was Joss's speculation. Casper didn't seem to have any issues with his teammates. He wasn't as standoffish as he had claimed, not even when they first met. He let him sit next to him and he was nice and fun when they hung out after leaving the club.

Casper wasn't as enthusiastic or exuberant as Demi, but he always contributed to the conversation. He was talkative when he wanted to be and smiled a lot when they video chatted. It could be that his teammates didn't know how to get along with Casper the way he struggled to get along with most of his own teammates. Lara and Natya made it easy, but he hadn't gotten to know the rest of the team well.

Thanksgiving dwindled down and he couldn't stay there forever. Every moment had an expiration date, and he was reaching it.

16: SURPRISE

Since coming back from Thanksgiving break, he worked harder. He stayed even later, having to practice while on a call with Casper and Demi. It didn't make it harder, but it was hurting his bullseye average. Sometimes it felt like they were hinting something just out of his reach which kept him distracted from trying to decipher their words. Things like: *Joss should have just stayed in his room while you visited. He always ruins everything.*

He thought they didn't get along with Joss, but maybe he was misinterpreting it?

They said goodnight to each other and Roman moved to stand in front of the ranking board. He was no longer on the bottom, but he and Haijun only had a two point difference between them and it could change the next day at practice. He stretched out his right arm, hoping it would help alleviate the pain. It had slowly been getting worse. If he told the team doctor he was worried, he would lose the progress he had been making, and he didn't want to bother them for a problem that a bit of ice and heat could fix.

To work on his blocker anxiety, he should be asking someone to stand in as a blocker instead of just doing target practice, but the only two teammates he got along with were runners. He didn't understand why most of the blockers seemed so intimidating. Cameron was probably the least scary of them all and maybe Yueying but she hung out with Silvana who was terrifying.

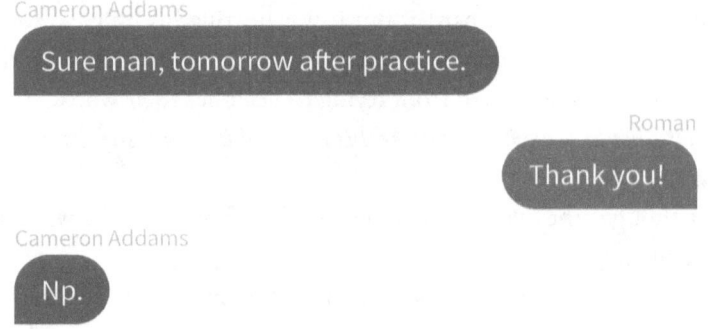

Roman

Hey, it's Roman. I was wondering if you had free time, if you wanted to… could you help me practice? I need someone to be a blocker but if you're busy no worries. Just let me know. Whenever it works for you.

Roman pressed send and wanted to smash his phone into the floor. It was a horrible text. A few minutes later he got a reply.

Cameron Addams

Sure man, tomorrow after practice.

Roman

Thank you!

Cameron Addams

Np.

He grinned, he finally had a plan. Feeling energized, he grabbed his arrows, put them back in the quiver and started to practice on different bunkers. He climbed the first one and shot at the left target. Bullseye. Then the middle target. Middle ring. The right target was too far from his angle, he adjusted and went back to the first target. He took shot after shot until all of the arrows were gone, then he gathered them up and went to the next bunker. Then the next.

His hand shook on the last arrow, it went wide and dropped to the ground. Pain radiated from his shoulder, he carefully climbed down the bunker and jogged to his bag for a bottle of pain meds. Throwing them into his mouth with a gulp of water. He grabbed an ice pack out the team's freezer and held it to his shoulder as he picked up the arrows and put everything away. Instead of running to the dorms, he walked and hoped his shoulder would feel better tomorrow.

The next day, he stayed after practice with Cameron.

"How do you want to do this?" Cameron asked. He hadn't changed out of their practice gear. Cameron's dark skin glistened with sweat, a lazy smile on his lips.

"Uh." Roman hadn't had many, if any conversations with him. "How about the middle blocker box and I'll try and get some points from you?"

"Cool, cool. I got about thirty minutes, is that enough time for you?"

"Yeah, that's good." He would take five minutes, let alone thirty.

"Cool." Cameron pulled on his helmet and moved to the middle blocker box with the blocker pad on his arm.

Roman weaved onto the field, leaned against a bunker and tugged an arrow from the quiver. He didn't waste time and moved toward Cameron, he slid against the angled bunker, lifted the bow and took aim at the edge of the target. Cameron lunged and skimmed the arrow enough to knock it off course and miss the target. Roman pulled back and moved to a different area and angle. He climbed a bunker and took aim from there, just barely hitting the top of the target but in a game it would count. Dropping to the ground, he continued his attack. Most shots missed, but a few slipped past Cameron's defenses. An alarm went off and Cameron tugged the helmet off.

"I gotta head out," he called out. "Not bad, man."

"Thanks," Roman said. His bow lowered and he yanked his helmet off. His shoulder was throbbing but he could ignore it, for now. After Cameron left, he grabbed the bottle of ibuprofen, and threw three into his mouth.

When he got back to the dorm, he put a heating pad on his shoulder while he typed up his homework. The pain had become more than an annoyance, it was becoming a problem. He couldn't stop though, he was going to get enough rest time with winter break coming up. They wouldn't have any practices until they came back in January.

For now, he had to keep pushing. He still wasn't a starting player and had barely rose a rank on the team board. He still wasn't good enough.

Maybe he would never be good enough. He had to try. If he didn't, then what was the point?

The season was nearly over. They would most likely make it into the playoffs, but it wasn't guaranteed. They had to win their next game to be sure. It was his last chance to show what he could do in a game before the playoffs.

The playoffs were a double elimination competition, if they lost two games, they were out. The first loss would drop them into the losers bracket, where they would have one chance to keep playing. They may only have two games to play and if he didn't prove he could play better than his teammates, then he may not play at all. And he would lose his scholarship for poor performance. Without his parents paying for his college and without the scholarship, he couldn't afford college. With how much his parents made, he wouldn't qualify for most scholarships.

He was going to get better. He just had to keep training and get the pain in his shoulder to stop. He needed something stronger, something that wouldn't just dull the pain, he needed something to stop it.

He ignored his shoulder and the flaring pain, he didn't want to acknowledge how long it had been hurting or how much he had been trying to cover it up. He didn't want to be benched or put on a medical leave or the worst thing that could happen, he could lose his scholarship. He could handle it. It was fine, he was fine.

After he showered and got dressed, he threw his bag over his shoulder and looked through his phone. There was one new message.

Unknown Number

How many?

17: Capybaras vs Foxes

December 9th

Haley: Hello, hello. Did you miss us?

Javonna: What's there to miss when they can listen to the backlog of episodes?

Haley: Why do you always ruin my intro? Welcome to the Whimsical Whims podcast. We are back with another evobe game and if you missed our other one, then welcome to our terrible masquerade of being commentators.

Javonna: That's a good way of putting it. Please do not expect any real commentating. I promise to try to be good, but no promises of actual quality.

Period 1 | 15:27 | Capybaras: 6 - Foxes: 9

Javonna: It's kind of fun to watch them run around like little mice, but with bows and arrows. Do you think we could teach mice to use bow and arrows?

Haley: The last thing I want to see is a rat with a weapon.

Javonna: That's fair.

> Period 1 | 11:56 | Capybaras: 10 - Foxes: 13

Haley: The Foxes are doing a pretty good job of keeping the lead.

Javonna: I think the Capys will catch up. I'm choosing to believe in the pink uniform.

Haley: I bet you an iced latte that the Foxes win.

Javonna: Add a sushi lunch and you have yourself a deal.

Haley: Fine. Foxes win, you buy me an iced coffee and bbq; if you win, you get an iced coffee and sushi.

Javonna: Ha! Deal! You all heard it—oh shit, someone got a penalty. Looks like the foxes hit one of the runners... number 8 of the Capys. That's rude. That's the captain!

Haley: Do you know how the penalty's work?

Javonna: No, but my trusty sheet here does. Okay for a head shot penalty: The player is taken off the field for 3 minutes and they play 4 against 3, that sounds fun.

Haley: Aw, off they go. Bye, bye, little fox, see you soon.

Javonna: So they stand on the Foxes' side where the players come in for substitutes. Like a little jail.

Haley: I mean, there's no bars or even walls, it's some paint on the ground.

Javonna: That they can't leave before time's up or it's another penalty.

Haley: Whatever.

> Period 2 | 17:43 | Capybaras: 26 - Foxes: 20

Javonna: Well, I don't want to brag too early.

Haley: We're not even halfway through the game! Don't you dare.

Javonna: You never listen to me, I just said—

Haley: Shh.

Javonna: Shh? We are literally here to talk!

Haley: Then say something useful.

Javonna: Hmm. Number 9 Wade got 3 points on a target against the middle blocker. Lamb, what a cute name, got a point against Aukes.

Period 2 | 6:02 | Capybaras: 34 – Foxes: 31

Haley: Foxes are taking a timeout, with two left. The Capys haven't taken one yet.

Javonna: They look like flowers, all huddled around the coach.

Haley: I'm not even going to respond to that.

Javonna: Rude.

Period 3 | 10:17 | Capybaras: 45 - Foxes: 48

Javonna: Come on Capys, you got this!

Haley: Yes! The Foxes take the lead with a 3-point shot from Aukes.

Javonna: Tate gets a point from Holt. Wade gets a point from Aukes and Hutches gets a point from Lamb. I can barely keep up.

Haley: Everyone is attacking pretty aggressively.

Javonna: They only have ten minutes left and it's the last game of the season. Not everyone makes it into the playoffs, y'know?

Haley: Oh, now you're an expert.

Javonna: It's common knowledge.

Haley: Shut up, you're reading off of a sheet.

Javonna: Can you stop exposing me?

Haley: When you stop annoying me.

Javonna: Impossible.

Haley: Well, you have your answer.

Period 3 | 00:00 | Capybaras: 62 - Foxes: 58

Javonna: A free iced coffee and sushi. Ah, life is good.

Haley: Shut up.

18: WINTER CAMP

Florida's winter air held a tepidity to it that contrasted with the frigid wind of Pennsylvania. It was easy to forget the chill when surrounded by warmth. It had only been a month since he last saw Casper, Demi, and Joss. The days had crept past like a snail traveling a thousand miles.

Casper and Demi had already sent him pictures of their arrival. He glanced around hoping to see them. Roman followed the group as they were guided to their cabin and texted back that he had also arrived. They passed a small grassy area between the road and the mess hall and a few buildings for arts and crafts. At the center of the camp was the lake, with cabins surrounding it. A few docks jutted from the edge of the lake.

Roman's group veered to the left, the girls veered to the right. The boys' path took them away from the buildings with the girls going past the buildings. Inside of the third cabin were several bunk beds, a bathroom and a shower room. The team spread out, several taking bottom bunks. Roman also chose a bottom bunk near the window, dropping his bag on the bed. They would be sharing the cabin with another team that hadn't arrived yet. He picked up the light brown camp shirt. The other team joining their cabin and the girls on their teams would wear the same color.

Casper

What cabin are you in?

Roman

3

Casper

Ours is 8, we'll head to yours.

Roman

Ok.

Roman abandoned his stuff and pushed opened the creaky door, letting it swing closed behind him. The lake glistened in the center of the camp, but he knew most of the activities were hidden in the trees. The smell of pine blended with the earthy muddy scent of the lake. Unfolding the map they had been given; he saw at least six trails leading to other sections. In the distance, Casper and Demi came into view. He waved with a bright smile on his face.

Demi smiled back, picking up his pace; Casper matched and surpassed him, spurring Demi to run faster. They reached and passed by him as they slowed down. Roman clapped.

"Who won?" Demi asked, brushing his hair back with a lazy smile.

"I did," Casper declared.

"Bullshit." Demi shook his head, looking at Roman. "Who won?"

"I did," Roman said. Even if they were just friends and never anything more, he had their attention for the moment. "What does the winner get?"

"What do you want?" Demi asked, leaning toward him, a smirk on his face.

"Whatever you're willing to give me." That was the truth. He would take scraps or crumbs, anything they offered he would take to hoard like a dragon.

"And if it was the world?" Demi said jokingly.

"Then I guess the world would be mine." He knew it was nonsense, but it filled him with a sense of comfort. "What are we doing first?"

"There's not much to do yet. Want to walk around a trail?" Demi asked.

The trail led into the woods and over a small bridge. His arms hung loose at his sides. Demi slipped his hand into his. Roman glanced away, biting his lip as his heart pounded in his chest. To distract from it, he pointed out plants and birds he found familiar from nature documentaries. Holding hands was something friends did, was something children did, it didn't mean a relationship.

The trail circled around and brought them to the other side of the lake. More teams were arriving, moving in groups to their cabins.

"Too bad we weren't matched up for cabins," Roman said wistfully.

Casper snorted. "It would have never happened. My cousin and parents want me to transfer to Thunder. I don't know why they thought pairing us up would work."

"Wait, you might transfer to Thunder?" Roman asked. A sense of dread and panic rose in his chest.

Casper shook his head. "No, it's not going to happen."

"Oh, okay. Good." Relief flooded his system, he could still transfer.

"Good?"

"I mean, if you wanted, I don't mean, like if um..."

Demi and Casper laughed.

"It's okay," Casper said, patting Roman's head. "I get it."

"Good," Roman said, though he wasn't entirely sure what he had even been talking about.

They dropped him off at his cabin. He was reluctant to say goodbye, but the week and day wasn't over yet. He could see them again later. Demi kissed his hand before letting him go. Roman fought a blush and lost. He scrambled into his cabin with Demi's laughter trailing away.

His hands shook, and he was thankful the cabin was empty. He felt like he was having a panic attack, except he was also floating. He stumbled to his bed, collapsing onto it.

His heart rate slowed, his emotions came down from the high. Despite Demi's cryptic actions, he didn't think he was actually interested in him romantically. Demi would probably be more straight forward if he was. Casper would be... Casper might be shy. He really had no idea how they act. If anything, Casper and Demi would probably be in a relationship, he was just a friend, a friend that they were comfortable with, kissing hands type of comfortable.

He groaned, slapping his head several times. Even if they were interested, they would lose interest in him. Even his own parents didn't care about him, how could he expect Casper and Demi to care about him?

Friendship was easy, a relationship took work. Work he had never really done before. He probably wouldn't even make a good boyfriend. If they did date...

Flipping over, he shoved the pillow over his head. He was teetering into delusional territory. He wasn't good at math, but statistically getting one person to like you was hard but two people... that had to be at least twice as hard.

The next morning, Roman sat alone by the lake on one of the short docks near his cabin, watching a few people kayak. The idea of moving somewhere deep into the woods etched itself in his heart. He jumped at the sound of a familiar voice behind him.

"Boo!" Demi yelled.

"We were looking for you," Casper admitted.

Roman tilted his head. "Did you have something in mind, or do you want to sit with me?"

Demi smiled, it was mischievous but soft. "We're going to make friendship bracelets or boyfriend bracelets whatever the case may be."

It was comments like that that caused Roman to be unsure of their relationship. It didn't stop the fluttering in his stomach, though.

Instead of questioning his words, he responded, "That sounds fun."

Demi held out his hand, Roman reached out, taking it and allowing Demi to help him up. Demi wrapped his arm around his shoulders with Casper on his other side. They made their way to a small cabin next to the mess hall, several white tables were set up with matching white chairs. Clear tackle boxes full of various styles of beads and colors of string were on every table. They took a table in the center for themselves. Demi didn't wait for the instructor, digging his fingers into the lettered beads. He grabbed white string, then plucked out three letters, each the first letter of their names.

Roman copied him, Casper dipping his fingers in after him. Roman shifted through the strings, deciding on black and white. There were a few sheets on the table with different variations of bracelets. Roman chose a simple design for his. Casper chose white beads and black string.

Demi made a few comments but overall they worked in silence, the chatter from other tables and people coming in and out filled the silence. Roman jumped when a hand came down on the table next to his hands, messing up his knot.

"Hello, I'm Ally," she said. Her long blonde hair brushed over his shoulder. "Let me know if you need any help." Her voice was high pitched and overly sweet.

"Thanks, we're good for now," Demi told her without looking up from his work.

She pulled away from the table. "Okay, I'll be around if you have any questions." She went to other tables and offered her help to them.

Roman returned his focus to his work, weaving the strands together. He wrapped the half done piece over his wrist, trying to find the middle. Adding a few more knots, he slid the three beads on. With the letter 'R' in the middle, his favorite place to be. All of the letters were separated by simple heart beads and knots.

They spent the next half hour working, when they finished, Casper latched his own onto Roman's left wrist. Demi took his, and Casper took Demi's. After swapping, Demi pulled their wrists together and took several pictures, even taking some outside while they walked through the woods. Demi stopped them periodically, to take pictures and selfies.

Three months ago, Hurricane Debby had swept through Florida, leaving several neighborhoods damaged. A day had been set aside to help with the cleanup. Roman joined the same volunteer group as Casper and Demi, while Joss ended up with Natya and a few others from the Capybaras. Roman stayed close to Casper and Demi as they began picking up debris.

Demi broke the silence. "I was thinking, you don't have anything to do for the rest of break, right?"

Roman looked over to make sure Demi was talking to him. Though the only other person he could be talking to was Casper.

"No."

"And you were telling us you like glassblowing and our campus has an open studio you could use," Demi said.

He was hinting at something that Roman wasn't grasping.

Casper sighed, exasperated. "Do you want to stay with us for the rest of the break?"

Roman replied without thinking, "Yes."

Thanksgiving break hadn't been long enough. He loved the idea of going back to Port Vista and spending more time with them. They wanted him around, they wanted to spend time with him. A smile broke out on his face.

Casper grabbed an empty brown box and headed off toward the middle of the blocked off street. Roman took his trash bag, and with his glove-covered hands, began filling it in earnest. He pocketed the small pieces of sea glass that he found. He could reuse it in glass blowing. It wasn't enough to make anything out of it, but he could blend it with other glass. It didn't take long to get into the routine and the hours passed by with them taking a half an hour break for lunch.

At five, the whistle blew, calling them back to the bus. They piled up their full and half full bags. Casper kept a hold on the brown box that rattled and clinked when he walked.

"What's in the box?" Roman asked, trying to peek inside, but Casper moved it out of his reach.

"Glass," Casper said.

Roman's gaze lifted to Casper's neutral expression. "Glass?"

Casper nodded. "For you to use for glassblowing."

Roman opened then shut his mouth, at a loss for words. He eventually stuttered. "Thank you." He couldn't stop the flutter of happiness that Casper gathered sea glass for him. Not many knew you could reuse sea glass for glassblowing.

"No need for thanks."

Roman wanted to wrap his body around them and just squeeze as tight as he could. He fisted the bottom of his shirt, his knuckles turning white. He forced his fingers to loosen as they settled into their seats on the bus. Roman was pushed to the window by Casper. They sat flush together from their shoulders to their knees. Casper radiated heat, Roman pressed back.

Later that night, Roman stared at the top bunk above him, sounds of snoring and shifting sheets created a melody with croaking frogs and crickets. Carefully, he crept out of his bed, tugging on his shoes and snuck out of the cabin. He wasn't afraid of getting in trouble, he was worried about bothering the others. Once outside he made his way toward the lake.

He chose a spot at the end of a short wooden dock, where the moon reflected on the calm water of the lake. The temperature had dropped to a chilling degree. The dark pink sweatshirt kept away most of the chill and it was still warmer than when they left Pennsylvania. Roman shivered as a breeze passed by, creeping across his neck. He tugged his hood up. The sound of footsteps forced him to whip his head around.

TJ didn't speak as he dropped next to him on the dock.

His heartbeat calmed at the sight of someone familiar. "Can't sleep?" Roman asked.

"I'm sleepwalking," he replied.

Roman let the conversation die, he didn't have much to say anyway. Their silence amplified the sounds of nature around them.

"Joss—He—" TJ didn't finish his thought.

TJ could be alluding to any number of things involving Joss. "You can ask whatever."

"Has he ever cheated on anyone?"

"No," Roman said. TJ sighed in relief. "He hasn't dated anyone to cheat on."

"Shit," TJ muttered.

"Do you think he's cheating?" Roman asked. A twinge of awkwardness ran through him. He never imagined he would ever be having this conversation with someone. Joss wasn't much of a relationship person, but it didn't mean he would never get into a relationship.

"No, not yet. The way he talks to people, he's always flirting and then he just stops, like he suddenly remembers he's not supposed to, and then he looks and me and I don't know."

"He likes you, a lot. I didn't know anything about you until we met."

TJ scoffed. "That's not usually a good thing."

"With Joss it is. I've heard about every sexual experience he's ever had. Except you, so he must really care about you."

"He must have a lot of sexual experience for that to be your baseline."

Roman shrugged. He didn't know what the average was. "He's a people person."

"That's the issue."

Roman crossed his arms, clenching his sweatshirt in his hands. "I'm sorry. For what little it's worth, I don't think he would cheat. He's more likely to ask about a threesome then sneak around with someone. He's pretty straightforward with stuff like that."

"Right." TJ didn't sound convinced.

Roman was awful at comforting people and didn't know the ins and outs of their relationship. He didn't want to overstep. He said what he thought would help, but didn't want to say anymore.

They sat together for a while, enjoying the fluttering of fireflies and mosquitos and the sporadic sounds of splashing from fish. The scent of bug spray lingered on his skin. TJ was a comforting companion. If a murderer came, then he just had to run faster than him.

The next day, Roman wandered through the woods, his hands tucked into his light pink Capybaras' sweatshirt, it was quiet in the early morning. His shoulders lifted up and down, he smiled, it was finally feeling better. Though he didn't want to think it was because he hadn't been shooting, but it was the truth.

He had already taken his usual morning jog and shower. There were only a few things he had explored alone in Harmony. He realized being alone wasn't so scary. Anxiety still paralyzed him, but he was pushing past it. A flicker of pride washed over him. He had been improving, at least in some parts of his life.

When he turned around and made his way back to his cabin, Jax intercepted him, dragging him towards the first group event of the day.

"Can I skip it?" Roman asked.

"Nope," Jax said, wrapping an arm around his shoulders and dragging him forward where they met up with Lara, Natya, and the rest of the team. They showed up like an ad during a movie that you paid not to have ads for.

"We only get to choose two people to represent the team in target shooting, you have to do it!" Lara said.

Roman swallowed his apprehension. He wanted to avoid aggravating his shoulder, but he didn't have an excuse to get out of it.

"I'm excited for the rope obstacle course, we're going to kick all of their asses!"

He searched the growing crowd for Casper and Demi, but they never arrived. Joss waved at him, and TJ gave a slight nod.

Luckily, they only had to shoot five arrows, and they had to aim for the bullseye, something he was familiar with. He tugged off his sweatshirt to show off his brown cabin shirt. The murmur of the crowd disappeared, and he took aim and watched the tip of his arrow hit the bullseye, then the next and next until he reached down and found his quiver empty.

"Damn," Jax muttered. "Have you always been this good at hitting bullseyes?"

Roman looked at the other targets, most hit bullseyes, paint splattered all around the small circle. But his only had splatter in a single spot. He had hit the same spot, five times in a row.

"If only he was good enough to do it in a game," Silvana muttered.

"Shut up," Lara said.

Roman shrugged, she was right. If he couldn't do it in a game then it was worthless.

Demi or Casper remained elusive in every event Roman was dragged to participate in. He mourned the loss of time with them. If they held the camp where winter raged on, then they would have to stay inside. Instead, the sun shined with a light breeze and it felt like spring.

He caught sight of several Dragons players. Keira, with her red hair in braids and a wide smile, had triumphantly yanked the flag from his waist, knocking him out of the game. She waved it in the air and cheered with Sumaiya Shea, who wore a lavender hijab under her pink cabin shirt. Meena Hays waved her own conquered flag, her pink shirt was cut up and tied in knots.

After getting out of the game, he could finally find the two people he wanted to spend time with. Demi sent him texts, leading him through the woods. If he hadn't been accosted by Jax, he could have checked his phone and found them earlier. Ten feet away, he saw color in a dense forest of brown and green. Casper and Demi's voices were a low hum among the wildlife. A stick snapped beneath his foot breaking the tranquil atmosphere.

"Roman?" Demi called out, similar to someone in a horror movie before they discovered it wasn't their friend but the killer.

He stretched out the silence for a few moments. "It's me."

A light green triangle hammock stretched out to three trees where Casper and Demi were relaxing. Roman stepped closer and wondered if this was where they had been hiding all day.

"Come on up," Demi said, patting the spot next to him.

Roman's brow creased, a skeptical frown on his face.

"It's fine, I promise."

He stepped closer, hesitantly pressing on it. Demi laughed, sitting up, he grabbed Roman's wrist and tugged him forward. Roman stumbled bracing himself over Demi. Roman tried to shift back but Demi held him close.

"Please don't punch me," Demi said. He leaned forward. Roman froze and then melted into the kiss. His soft lips tasted like vanilla chapstick.

Roman pulled away biting at his bottom lip; he looked at Casper, then at Demi, and back to Casper. Casper reached out an arm and Roman half crawled over Demi to reach him.

"I'm not mad about this position," Demi commented.

Casper tasted like the same vanilla chapstick that Demi did. In the back of his mind, he wondered how many times they had shared chapstick and how many times they would share with him.

The quickly setting sun forced them to abandon the hammock, before leaving them to navigate the forest by cellphone light. They dropped Roman off at his cabin and continued on their own, with the promise of spending more time together tomorrow.

Roman pulled the blanket over his head. He wanted them to like him, they might not if they knew he was asexual. Just because he wasn't interested in it didn't mean he couldn't do it. For them he could find an interest, at least he could try to. Like eating something he didn't care for. He could eat it, he just normally wouldn't choose it on the menu, but if someone chose it and wanted to share with him, he wouldn't say no. They made him feel wanted, and it wasn't a feeling he was willing to let go. Even if it wasn't a relationship. Even if this was just something fun for them, he wanted it. He was tired of feeling unwanted, unloved, unworthy.

19: HOME

The rest of the team decided to go to Vermont for the rest of winter vacation. It was only Roman, Demi, Casper, their coach, the assistant coach, and the manager on the bus back to Port Vista. They played musical bus seats until the coach yelled at them to knock it off. Roman stayed in his seat for the rest of the drive, ignoring Casper and Demi's teasing.

Going back to Port Vista was like going home, it was a strange feeling since it wasn't his home. The dorm was blissfully quiet without other students, if he thought too much about it, the silence would become eerie, desolate, isolating.

Demi laughed as he pushed open the dorm door. "We're home!" he called out.

We're home. It could mean nothing. It could just mean him and Casper. He hoped it included him too, even if it wasn't really *his* home.

Roman woke up early the next morning, immediately wanting to use the sea glass Casper gathered for him. He grabbed a muffin for breakfast on his way to the hot shop for the public session he signed up for with the encouragement from both of them. His fingers trembled and his stomach turned. It had been months since he went into the studio. He almost giggled walking in the door. The hot shop smelled like burning newspaper and life. Since he started glassblowing at fifteen, he had never taken more than a week's worth of break from making glass. Drawing had helped him fill the creative void, but for him, it couldn't compare to glass.

"Hello, are you Roman?" A woman stepped out of an office. Her blonde hair was up in a tight bun, she reminded him of Lara, except sweet looking.

"That's me," he said.

She smiled shyly. "Good, otherwise this would be awkward. Have you done this before, or is this your first time?"

"I've done it before."

"Okay, do you need help or an instructor?"

"No, I can work by myself."

"Great, if you change your mind, let me know. I'm Gwen, by the way. You'll have two hours. If you need more time, just tell me." Her fingers, with light sparkling pink nail polish, pinched together. "It will be a small charge for extra time."

"I understand."

"Wow, this is easy. There are tools over there. Everything has labels, but if you can't find anything, then—"

"Let you know," he interjected. He had done this dance many times before.

"Exactly."

Setting the box of glass from Casper on an empty bench, he fluttered around the wall of tools, gathering what he needed. He took a few moments to breathe in the scent of fire and newspaper, to soak in the heat. Then he focused on his sketch. Tapping the pencil on the paper, he couldn't think of what to create. The moment he was waiting for presented itself and his mind was blank.

Time ticked forward on a large digital clock. The red numbers were mocking him. He wasted twenty minutes on staring at a blank page. The box was full of different colored glass. He pulled several pieces out hoping they gave him inspiration. He lifted the glass to the light, stacked them on top of each other and finally he fell back into the old ways when he had nothing to do.

He made orbs, paper weights, pretty balls of glass. It was like swimming after not being in a pool for years, his body remembered every step he was supposed to take.

At the end of the two hours he finished two orbs, one black with swirls of green and one white with swirls of red, he placed them in the annealer to cool and to come back for later.

The campus was still deserted on his way back to the dorms. He unlocked the door with the temporary key given to him. Casper was on the couch reading a book, while Demi's singing voice poured out of the bathroom with the shower running.

"How was it?" Casper closed his book, giving his attention to Roman.

"It was nice." Roman kicked off his shoes, setting the key on the bar counter. "I'm going to go back later and pick it up." He dropped onto the other side of the couch. "What are you reading?"

Casper lifted the book shoving off the red and black cover. "I just started it, it's interesting so far."

Roman smiled. "Lara really likes fantasy books too. She actually said she thought you read business books for fun."

Casper frowned. "Is that what I seem like?"

Roman's shoulder lifted in a half shrug. "I don't think so." He looked Casper up and down. He was in a simple white T-shirt and black shorts, with a relaxed slouch. "Maybe because you seem serious all the time?"

"Do I seem serious?" Casper's face contorted.

Roman chuckled. "I think that's the perception people have of you, and I think you do it on purpose."

"I do. I've gotten so used to having a neutral persona that I don't know how to stop it."

He tilted his head. Thinking back to Joss's words at Thanksgiving. "You're not like that with me or Demi."

"Because I trust you and him, even if he can be an asshole."

He hadn't seen Demi be an asshole, not yet at least. Maybe he did like to push people's buttons a little too much, but he was just teasing, mostly.

"When I was younger, the paparazzi and news outlets were interested in my family, looking for a scandal or just any piece of news. Stories came out twisting every facial expression I had. When my parents started to really make money, some people campaigned against us. I didn't grow up rich, we were middle class and supporting my aunt and cousin. I was a normal kid, going to school with friends and I know it was months if not years before it all changed, but it felt like it was overnight. My school changed, my parents didn't trust any of my friends, we got a bigger house, they weren't home anymore, and every time I left the house someone was taking a picture of me or them. I hated the money. It changed everything. I used to love evobe, but it's become a cage I haven't been able to escape."

Roman leaned forward, wrapping his arms around Casper. His fingers tightened on Casper's soft shirt.

"I'm calling foul!" Demi called out.

He jumped and let go of Casper. Demi walked out of the bathroom shirtless, water dripping from his hair with a teasing grin on his face.

"So what was I interrupting?"

Casper didn't play into Demi's teasing. "What are we doing for lunch?" Casper asked.

"Whatever you want," Demi said, not caring about the change of topic.

Roman fidgeted, it was becoming harder to ignore the comments and strange atmosphere. No one was saying anything about making out or doing it again. Were they forgetting it ever happened, or was he just not understanding something?

"Since we're changing topics, can we talk about our relationship?" Roman asked. "Just um, to clarify?"

Demi rubbed the back of his neck. "I guess we haven't done that, have we?"

The silence stretched beyond what Roman was comfortable with. He twisted his fingers. His eyes darting between them. Maybe this was a mistake. *He shouldn't have said anything.*

Casper chuckled. "It doesn't have to be complicated, we all like each other, right?"

Roman nodded slowly, still unsure if they were all on the same page or not. Liking someone didn't always equate to more than a friendship.

"I kinda thought we were doing an unspoken change of relationship," Demi said. "So boyfriends?"

"Boyfriends," Roman agreed. It was one word, but it changed everything and nothing. All the delusions shattered. All the fear of not being liked evaporated. They liked him. They *liked* him. They liked *him*? He dug his blunt nails into his palms until it hurt. He wasn't asleep, he was awake, this was real.

Later that day, they went out shopping for dinner and a shelf where they displayed the two orbs that Roman made for them. The shelf was better than any gift, they wanted a special place to show his work, he didn't have to hide it in his closet. Here it was on display and it meant the world to him.

Roman rolled his shoulders back. The break from evobe and practices had worked wonders on his shoulder pain. He grabbed the borrowed bow and tugged an arrow from the quiver, aiming at the target in front of him.

"Have you thought about shooting around the target?" Casper asked.

Roman's aim faltered. He glanced at Casper. "What do you mean?"

"Well, you can obviously hit your target. You proved that. What if you change your target?"

"Change my target to the outside?"

"Points are points. Why waste an arrow on a bullseye that's heavily blocked, when you could get points by hitting the edge of a target?"

Roman stared at the target in front of him. He had been so focused on the bullseye, too focused. He lifted the bow, yanked back the string and released the arrow. It hit the edge of the target.

"In a game, that's three points," Casper said.

He was right. Why had he been so focused on the bullseye? That was the most guarded area of a target because an entire person stood in front of it. Aiming for the edge of the target, there was always a chance. The blocker could be a bit slow or not reach far enough to knock it away. If he could gain points this way, he could be a starting player. He just had to be consistent. Which meant he needed to practice a lot. His shoulder twitched at the thought. If he made it work, they may even make it to the finals.

20 : 17%

The start of the new semester was a breath of fresh air. He also had no classes on Fridays and took two less classes to avoid overloading his schedule.

The day after winter break ended, Jax gathered everyone into the common room.

"I hope everyone enjoyed their break. We'll be having night practices Monday, Tuesday, and Wednesdays, and morning practice on Saturdays." A round of groans sounded from the group.

"I know, I know, let's just be happy we have our Saturday nights empty, okay? I'm sure most of you have seen the viral post about the Dragons?"

"Are we going to do it too?" Lara asked.

"I think we should. Anyone who wants to op-out is welcome to. I brought some paper for people who want to join in."

Roman had seen it. Casper and Demi had done their own video since they weren't with the rest of the team in Vermont. Someone had posted photos of Alishba Shea from the Dragons with her girlfriend Marcella Aukes from the Foxes. Causing a scandal where there really wasn't one. Articles were posted about how evobe was breeding sexuality. The Dragons posted a video, and several other teams had already posted their solidarity.

He stared at the blank paper, it would be so easy to just write straight or gay or even bisexual. He didn't have to be truthful, but he didn't want to lie. His hand moved and he wrote sexual first. He could always add *Bi* or he could write the truth and add an *A*. Tapping the marker on the paper, thoughts swirled and jabbed at his brain. He wasn't ashamed of who he was, he had accepted it years ago, he even felt like maybe he and Joss were opposites that canceled each other out. It was the uncertainty of what other people would think that held him back. He just didn't know if he was ready for the team or Casper and Demi to know. Most people thought asexual meant he couldn't have sex. But he could, he just wasn't interested in it. He could go the rest of his life without having sex, but he was willing and able to do it for his partner or partners.

He took the offered paper and wrote *He/him* and added an *A* on the sheet, he supposed he wouldn't be able to hide it from Casper and Demi anymore. He didn't want to hide it forever, especially now that they were officially boyfriends. Now was probably the best time to tell them.

Two days later, on Thursday, he woke up with his head pounding, vision cloudy and he was freezing. He cocooned into his blanket, but it was a Band-Aid on a broken bone, useless. Shivers wracked his body, tightening his grip on the blanket. He coughed, his throat was dry and scratchy. Sticking a hand out, he searched for his water bottle.

A blaring alarm sounded from his phone and he quickly shut it off. Sunlight spilled into the room, his eyes narrowing at his water bottle on his desk. Taking a deep breath, he threw the blanket away. He knew he was sick, but he couldn't miss class or practice. He chugged his water, pulled on a sweatshirt, a black coat and shoes and threw his backpack over his shoulder.

He took a breath of fresh air and began coughing. Covering it with a medical mask, he made his way to class. He didn't know why everyone was walking so quickly. It was as if everyone was late. Roman checked his phone. The night before, he had been tired and forgot to plug his phone it was at seventeen percent. He shoved it back in his pocket, ducked his neck into his coat and forced himself to keep walking. He ignored the messages on his phone, his head hurt too much to read. He saw one text that finally allowed for some relief.

> Practice is cancelled until Monday. Everyone is sick, if anyone needs anything let me know.

His eyelids became heavy, but he made it through the torturous Thursday and with a bowl of ramen he went back to his dorm and bed. When he finally had a moment to relax, he remember his phone. Plugging it in, it turned on and buzzed with notifications.

Steam billowed up from the bowl of ramen, the broth soothed his scratchy throat. The smell of chicken and spices couldn't penetrate through his stuffed nose.

Buzz Buzz. Roman answered his ringing phone.

"Hello?"

"Roman? Are you okay?" Demi's exuberant voice called out.

Roman hummed, his head leaning against the wall. "Sick," he muttered.

"Shit, do you need me to do anything?"

"No, I'm going to eat and then sleep."

"Take some medicine and text me when you feel better."

"Mhm."

The phone fell to the side and another sip of broth slipped down his throat until all that was left was noodles and meat. He set the bowl on his shelf, slumped over and fell asleep.

Roman groggily opened his eyes, someone was pounding on his door.

"Roman? Hello?" More pounding. "If you don't unlock the door, I'm going to use the spare key and make sure you're not dead."

It took a while for Roman to parse out Jax's voice. He rolled off of the bed, his bones were like jelly when he tried to stand up. The door swung open, and the light from the hallway burned his eyes.

"So you are alive, you have a delivery."

"Delivery?" Roman choked out.

"Looks like you have it pretty bad too. Lara said she saw you leave this morning, so I thought you were safe from the sickpocolypse." Jax's voice was slightly muffled from the mask he wore. He pushed a box on the floor closer to Roman.

In the box was six tall containers of soup, two packages of breadsticks all from a restaurant, and a variety of medicine that could put a pharmacy to shame.

"Am I supposed to choose?" Roman leaned on the doorway.

"Nope, this all came for you."

"Is everyone getting one?" Roman didn't understand why he was getting a care package. Not even his own parents helped him when he was sick, they didn't want to get contaminated and possibly get others sick, so he was always put in quarantine in his room.

"I'm pretty sure it just came for you."

"I don't understand."

"From a Casper and Demi?" Jax lifted and lowered the card repeatedly. "Wait, Casper and Demi? Like from the Dragons?"

Roman grabbed two breadsticks and a few of the medicines, tea, honey, and lemons. "Give the rest to whoever needs it, if no one needs it, can you put it in the fridge?"

"Can do."

"Thanks." He crawled back to bed and munched on the buttery garlic breadsticks. It didn't fix his headache or his stuffy nose, but it did mend the thought that he would always have to take care of himself, even if he was sick.

Roman

Are you alive or dying from whatever is going around?

Lara

Dying, dead. I'm undead now. How are you?

> **Roman**
> Not undead but not far from it. Jax is handing out soup and some breadsticks.

> **Lara**
> Remind me to make him an altar.

> **Roman**
> I'll screenshot this and send it back to you.

> **Lara**
>

Friday dawned late, Roman woke up to the sound of Jax poking his head in. "Want me to heat up soup for you? Or anything else?"

"Tea and honey, please?"

"No problem."

He sent several ugly selfies to Casper and Demi with the tea and soup to thank them. It wasn't good enough but until he was better, it was all he could do.

On Sunday, everyone began to feel better and life resumed its monotonous party.

Mid-January brought a storm that rattled the windows and snow fell endlessly. Jax had called all of them into the common room, telling them classes and practice were cancelled for the next few days. Someone suggested a movie, Roman squished into his chosen chair, reading through his texts from Joss, Casper, and Demi. Joss was complaining that winter break didn't last long enough, while Casper and Demi were arguing about spending time with the team.

Demi

> You can bring a book and ignore everyone like normal.

Casper

> If I'm going to ignore everyone anyway, then I might as well stay home.

Demi

> It won't kill you to be there.

Casper

> It won't kill you for me to stay home.

Demi

> Roman, tell him he should spend time with his teammates.

Roman

> I'm spending time with my teammates.

Demi

> If Roman can do it then you can too.

Silviana's high voice rose. "Oh, I'm not a team player? Fuck off. What about Wade? He never says anything and pretends we don't exist. Does anyone even know his first name?" Silviana complained.

"It's Roman," Nayta said.

"You know what I mean! Anyone know anything else about him?" Silviana stood, her hand thrown toward him.

The room was quiet, and everyone turned their attention to him.

Roman glanced down at his phone as is vibrated in his hand and then back up to everyone still staring.

"See! He can't even speak! So, don't come barking at me that I'm not a team player when that fucker has been here the whole time and no one even fucking cares about him."

Roman opened his mouth, he wanted to argue to say something, but words failed him. She wasn't wrong, but he also didn't know what they were fighting about.

"I can talk," Roman said. He felt stupid as soon as the words were out of his mouth.

Silviana glared at him. "Good for you! I don't care! I really don't fucking care."

"Okay, okay, you made your point you can calm down," Jax said.

"Fuck off. I'm not dealing with this bullshit." She stomped out of the room.

"I mean, she isn't wrong," Mariona commented. Her arms crossed over her red sweatshirt.

"That's not fair," Lara said. "It's not like you're the pinnacle of team bonding."

Mariona snorted, her straight nose scrunched up. "Oh, here comes perfect Lara in for the rescue."

"Don't come at me because you have your own problems."

"I have problems?" She pointed to herself, then sat up from her spot on the couch.

Lara raised an eyebrow. "You think you don't? How about that girl I saw you fucking last week? She has a boyfriend, but you don't care about that, right? You only go after people with significant others."

Mariona stood up, charging for Lara. Jax and Pio intercepted her.

Lara stood as well, her blonde hair flowed around her. "No, let her go. What are you going to do, hit me? Try it. Please hit me. You can punch and scratch your scholarship away."

"You're a fucking bitch!" Mariona screeched.

"At least I don't have the morals of a dumpster. You'll just take anything thrown your way, won't you?"

Mariona kicked and thrashed against Jax and Pio who struggled with holding her back.

"Can someone help? Lara, fucking leave!" Jax yelled.

A few others jumped up to help. Roman skimmed the edge of the room and made his way out. Mariona called him a coward, but he ignored it and sped up to reach his room.

An hour later, Roman opened his door just a crack, peeking out. No one was in the hallway, he quickly raced across to the bathroom. He went as quickly as he could and rushed back into his room. The first thing he did was call Demi.

"How did it start?" Demi asked.

Roman frowned. "I don't know."

"Who was it about before they yelled at you?"

"I don't know. Silvana was yelling first, and then Lara and Mariona started yelling at each other."

Demi sighed with a shake of his head. "I should have been there, next time pay attention to the details. No, better yet, record it and send it to me. Then I'll see it for myself."

"Is it really that interesting?" he asked.

"Yes, and it kills me that you don't think so."

Roman scrubbed at his face. "I don't think anyone will react well to me recording an argument."

"That's true. Are you having that much trouble being friends with them?"

Roman tugged his pillow into his lap. "Sort of. I'm just used to Joss. With Joss as my friend, I didn't really have to care about anyone else."

"But it's easy with us, right?"

"Yeah, but you make it easy, and so does Lara. I just—I don't know. I don't know how to make friends, I guess."

Demi laughed. "We did sort of force our friendship on you. Kind of. Alcohol probably helped. You were pretty talkative."

"Was I?"

Demi hummed. "Maybe you all just need to drink together. What better time to do it than being stuck inside together?"

"I don't know if that's a good idea. What if they're still fighting?"

"Then it's more drama and fun for me or they figured it out last night and everything is fine."

Roman groaned. He hadn't been in a lot of fights, but he didn't think it would resolve itself.

Casper stepped up behind Demi. "You don't have to do anything. You can keep being your normal self and eventually get to know them or never do."

"Or you could take a chance and maybe make some friends," Demi said, pushing Casper away.

"I like Casper's suggestion," Roman muttered.

"See? He's fine, leave him alone," Casper said as he left the screen.

"He asked for help. I'm not forcing him to do anything," Demi complained.

Demi was right, though. He didn't have any problems with the team; instead, he felt inferior to them. He was the one who struggled to grasp the plays, he was the one who was being distant. He was supposed to be good, he had gotten in, he was on the same field as them, in the same uniform and yet, he felt like an elementary student compared to them.

The next morning, he stepped out into the hallway and then stared at the kitchen. Demi was always talking about how food brought people together. Stepping forward, he got to work, making a massive pile of pancakes. They had orange juice but no champagne, but he found a bottle of Moscato wine. He made imitation Mimosas, brought everything to the common room, then he knocked on everyone's door.

"If this is an apology, then I accept," Mariona said, spraying whipped cream on top of her pancakes.

"Thanks," he murmured. He didn't feel like he owed an apology to anyone, but if the fight was really caused by him, then he supposed this was an apology.

Lara elbowed his side. With a smile she moved toward the coffee table to grab her own plate of pancakes.

"Thanks for sticking up for me," he told her.

She winked. "It was fun."

He knew this didn't fix everything, but he could do more to be a part of the team. Even if he didn't feel like he deserved it, they all wore the same uniform.

21: Birthday Boy

Roman thought the gap between Thanksgiving and winter break was hard, but seeing Casper and Demi for most of winter break made being separated that much harder. Instead of wallowing in it, he put more effort into working hard. He added an extra mile to his runs and another fifty arrows to target practice. When he finally got into a good routine the ache returned to his shoulder, he just wasn't strong enough yet.

Roman propped his phone up as the call continued to ring. He snuggled down into his pillow, yawning as it connected and Demi and Casper appeared on screen.

"Hi," Roman said sleepily.

"Should I start reading you a bedtime story?"

Roman smiled. "I'm sorry, I keep falling asleep." He didn't want to attribute it to the pills he had to take to keep the shoulder pain at bay, but it was a contributing factor.

"Don't be sorry. We understand, besides, I like seeing your sleeping face."

Roman tried not to cringe with worry about what he looked when he was asleep. Exhaustion was too much and as expected, Roman fell asleep on the video call. His days were long, but he never wanted to miss a video call with his boyfriends.

The next morning, a notification popped up from the calendar in his phone. It was almost Casper's birthday. He searched online what to get him, but he still had no idea. The internet told him to get him: a candle, towels, cologne, or sex.

Casper smelled faintly of honey whiskey, subtle enough that Roman didn't want it to change. He spun around in his desk chair, wanting to find him something he'd actually like. They usually talked about books, so Roman sat up and opened his computer, searching for gifts for readers. None of it seemed right, it was all just knick-knacks that he didn't need. He sighed. He should just ask Demi.

Switching his search to long-distance relationships, he still came up with nothing. Roman set his phone down. Instead of guessing, he should ask him. But then it wouldn't be a surprise, but what use was a surprise if the person didn't like it? He folded his arms, laying his forehead against them. It was easier when he only had to go out to eat with Joss and give him a box of condoms. Maybe if he put together small things, it could turn into a good big thing.

Casper's birthday list: Condoms? Size? Flavor? A book? Snacks? Candle?

Roman strolled through the store looking for something to put Casper's gifts in. He stared at the Easter baskets made up as Valentine's Day baskets. He looked for something else to fill up.

The airport was packed with travelers, some were comfortable with blankets over them and their legs stretched out. Others were on the floor with phones plugged into wall outlets. The screen shifted with updates, ON TIME announcements shifted to DELAYED. Outside of the large ceiling to floor window, snow poured down as wind whipped it around creating a snow globe effect.

Roman found one open seat next to a family and a couple. It was still early, he left right after class ended, hoping his flight would leave before the storm hit. The minutes ticked down and some flights shifted from

DELAYED to CANCELED. Two hours later, DELAYED switched to BOARDING.

A cool wind blew in, caressing his neck and forcing him to shiver. He paced outside of the dorm building, it was late. He was supposed to get in at seven and now it was nearly midnight. He couldn't stay outside for the entire night, and he nearly unintentionally ignored Casper all day besides a happy birthday in the morning and his birthday was now nearly over. Tugging his phone out of his pocket, he called Demi.

"My favorite person, hello."

"Hi, um, what are you doing?"

"Just lying in bed with the birthday boy, want to video chat?"

"Actually, I sent something for Cas. It says it was just delivered. Can you go grab it for him?"

Sounds of shuffling came from the other side of the phone. "Yep, getting up now."

"Thanks."

Roman pulled up his hood, set the laundry basket down at his feet, and quietly cleared his throat.

The door pushed open, and Demi nearly jumped.

"Sorry, I think this is mine."

"I need a signature from Casper Graves."

Demi paused, tilted his head and narrowed his eyes. "You little trickster."

Roman laughed. "Was my voice really obvious?"

"Yeah, that and I'm still on the phone with you."

"Oh."

Demi straightened up and hugged him. "Is that a laundry basket?"

"It's Casper's gift, well, his gifts are in it. Don't ask me how I got it on the plane. I was also supposed to get in earlier, but the flight was delayed."

The basket was filled with random gifts. Some were thought out and others were impulsive choices.

Demi laughed, ruffled his hair, and lifted the basket. "Come on, he's going to love this."

Demi led him into the dorm. Casper was on the couch in a loose black T-shirt and boxers.

"What did you have to go out—" Casper's voice cut off as he stood.

Roman kicked off his shoes and waved his hands. "Surprise. Happy Birthday."

Casper wrapped him in a hug, Roman leaned into, soaking in his warmth and the scent of honey whiskey. It was a sharp sweet scent. Casper pulled back, kissed his temple, and let go.

Roman's cheeks flushed, an awkward smile gracing his lips.

"Thank you," Casper murmured.

"He brought gifts," Demi said, lifting the basket.

"I may have panicked. And then there was a ton of stuff for Valentine's Day and I just grabbed a bunch of stuff."

"I forgot about Valentine's Day," Demi said. "Are we celebrating that?"

"I'm okay if we don't," Roman said. He had enough things to panic and worry about.

"Let's skip it then," Casper decided. "It's late. Do you want to get ready for bed?"

"Is Joss here or at TJ's?"

"TJ's. You can stay in his room... Or you could stay in mine," Casper said.

"Do you want me to stay in your room?"

Casper smiled. Usually, it was smaller and gentle, but this one was wide and playful. "Yes. Of course I do. I would keep you here If I could."

"That would be kidnapping," Demi said.

Casper's smile slipped into something more sarcastic as he glanced at Demi, but Roman still loved it.

"It's not if he agrees. And it would be imprisonment. He brought himself here. I would just be keeping him here."

Demi nodded. "It's not the worst idea you've had. Where's your phone? We should ditch it in a dumpster somewhere."

Roman laughed. They wouldn't have to force him to stay. He wished he never had to leave.

It was late, he brushed his teeth, changed into comfy clothes and gingerly crawled into Casper's bed. When he stayed over winter break, he had stayed in Joss's room. Roman twisted his shirt with his fingers, unsure if they just wanted to go to bed or if they were expecting something else. Casper crawled onto the inside against the wall, while Demi took the outside. They both gave him a goodnight kiss and then that was it.

Roman stared at the ceiling, disappointment and relief warred in his mind. It had been long a day and it didn't take long before his eyes drifted shut. They opened again as Casper's arm wrapped around his waist. It took a while before he relaxed and started to fall asleep again.

The next morning, Roman woke up alone. He glanced around and found his phone plugged in on the side table. It was already nine, he didn't usually sleep in. Rolling out of bed, the dorm was empty. In the kitchen he found a plate of pancakes wrapped up with his name on them. As they heated up, he texted Joss.

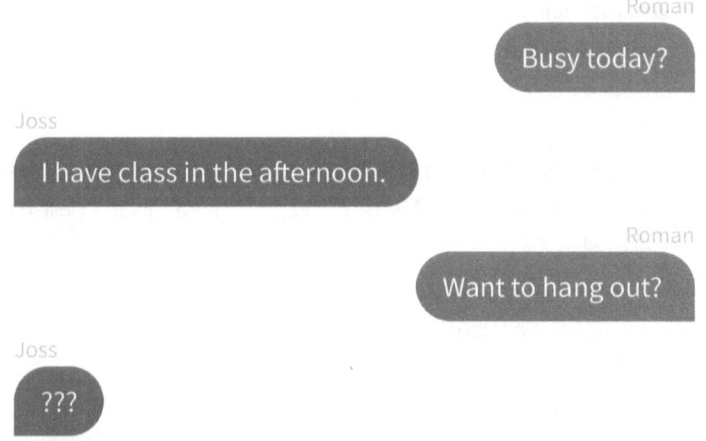

Roman

> Busy today?

Joss

> I have class in the afternoon.

Roman

> Want to hang out?

Joss

> ???

An hour later, Joss and Roman relaxed on a gray couch in TJ's dorm. The dorm looked nearly the same as Casper and Demi's, excepted it was mirrored. TJ's place was meticulously cleaned without any type of clutter. It made Roman hesitant to make a mess with his presence alone.

"I think I'm starting to feel offended that you're not here to visit me," Joss said over the sound of the movie playing.

"It's Casper's birthday."

"You didn't visit on my birthday."

"Did you want me to?" Roman asked, turning his head to look at him.

Joss shrugged. "It would have been nice."

"I'm sorry, I'll be with you on the next one." Roman thought for a few moments. "I was with you on your birthday. Your birthday isn't until March."

Joss grinned, his eyes crinkling. "It took you way too long to realize that."

"You're so annoying," Roman groaned.

"You never used to say things like that," Joss said. "I think I'm starting to feel jealous that Ghost and Demon are stealing all of your attention. They better not be trying to steal my spot as your best friend."

Roman stared at Joss without responding, besides it being weird hearing Casper and Demi's nicknames, Joss was being sincere.

"What? I'm being serious."

"I know. It's weird." In all of their time being friends, they only had a few serious sincere conversations.

"Why?"

Roman shrugged. Sometimes he saw glimpses of a genuine Joss and every time it surprised him. "No one is replacing you as my best friend. They're different."

This time Joss froze. "Different? Like how?"

"Like more than a friend."

"With who?"

"Cas and Demi."

"Since when?" Joss's eyes narrowed as he leaned toward him.

"It's only been a few weeks."

"Why didn't you say anything?"

"Why didn't you say something about TJ?"

142

Joss shifted back. "I like him. I nearly love him. Maybe I love him. I don't fucking know. And I did tell you."

Roman stood up, filled with restless energy. "After I asked you about it."

He paced in front of the TV. It had been so long since he had a real conversation with Joss, where they talked about everything going on. "I like them. I love when they call me. I love waking up and seeing texts from them. I love that they will video call me and we just do our own thing, but they're right there."

Roman stopped and looked at Joss who was smiling at him. His tone softened, less crazed. "I love when I have a bad day and they send me take out. I love that they try to take care of me. I love that they make me want to do better. I love that when we're together, they focus on me and what I want. And I really just love learning things about them." He dropped onto the couch, staring at the movie.

"I learned that I can love a lot. I thought I could just accept any kind of love, but I can't. I want to be wanted. I want to feel loved and cared about. I feel like they care about me." His throat was dry. If he continued to speak he would choke.

"I'm going to need five to seven business days to process that confession," Joss said.

Roman rolled his eyes.

"Joking, it's good. No, it's great that they make you feel loved. I guess I feel shitty that I never let you feel that way."

Roman dropped his head against the couch. "I feel like everything is different."

"Why? You want to spit in each other's hand, shake, and promise to always be friends?"

Roman shrugged. "Maybe it would help." He rolled his head to the side to glance at Joss.

"Give me your hand. I'll spit in it right now." Joss tossed his right hand out.

Roman crossed his arms. "I'm serious."

Joss narrowed his eyes as if contemplating grabbing his hand. "Shit's supposed to change. Look, we're here, right? My phone is always on. Call me, text me. Whenever you want."

That offer had always been on the table. Roman had just been waiting for a text to go unanswered. He could reach out anytime he wanted. Why was he always waiting for Joss to do it?

Roman never felt like a priority to Joss. At least not while they were with other people. It was nice to hear and see Joss, but their dynamic had changed drastically since they left for college. Even if they had gone to the same college, he knew it would have changed. They had been on the same sidewalk in middle and high school, but college had created open roads for them. They left that sidewalk behind. It was nice to visit, but they couldn't remain contained to it.

"Knock knock," Demi said, standing at the open door of TJ's dorm.

"You hurt him, you die," Joss said. It was the most casual threat Roman had ever heard.

"Hurt him like how? Having him sign his soul over?" Demi asked seriously before breaking into a grin. "No worries from us. Should I give the same warning for TJ?"

Roman smiled, it seemed Demi played into the demon rumors.

"Fuck off," TJ called out.

"I guess not." Demi shrugged. "Ready?" he asked, looking at Roman.

"Yep." Roman stood up, and as he left, he thought about everything TJ had overheard them talk about. He supposed it didn't matter, he hadn't said anything about their chat on the dock, he figured TJ wouldn't talk about his strange confession.

Later that night, anxiety flooded his body. He lifted his phone after it vibrated with a text.

Joss

I forgot to ask, have you had sex with them yet?

Flipping his phone over, he pretended the text didn't exist. Roman bit his lip, his fingers tapping on the slightly sticky surface. The drink in front of him was half-drunk. He needed it. He had agreed to this little game, but that didn't make it any less nerve-wracking.

The bar he was in was busy but not packed. It was geared more toward locals than college students, but that didn't mean there weren't a plethora of them anyway.

"Hey, can I buy you a drink?"

Roman startled at the strange voice. This was all Demi's idea, but he didn't know if a real stranger was also part of the plan. Demi hadn't said anything about it.

"Uhh..." He hesitated. Casper was supposed to ask him that.

A warm body leaned up against his back. He almost jumped forward in case it was another stranger, but he recognized the hand pushing a drink forward.

"No, he doesn't," Casper said, his lips brushing against Roman's ear. The stranger left, but Casper remained pressed against his back. "You never know what kind of strangers you'll meet in a bar."

Roman licked his lips, glancing at the fresh drink on the table. He could do this; he just had to pretend to be someone else.

"I-uh..." Roman choked out.

"Need a drink?" Casper asked in a smooth voice.

He chugged the rest of his drink, then started on the one Casper brought.

"You don't have to rush," Casper chuckled.

Roman set the drink down as Casper's hands slipped over his waist. Demi had dressed him in tight jean shorts, luckily not the shortest pair that was offered, but they were still too tight and short for his liking. He sucked in a breath when Casper's chilled hand slipped under the slight crop top. He grabbed the drink and pretended the chills across his body were from the cold drink.

"Do you have a boyfriend?" Casper asked.

The alcohol was slowly sinking in, not as quickly as he would like, but he just needed to pretend. Roman turned in Casper's arms, smirking. His back was pressed against the table. "And what if I did?"

"Just makes it more thrilling."

"And what makes you..." Roman's mind stuttered. "Um... What makes you think I would be interested in you?"

Casper didn't respond; instead, his hand rose to his neck. Roman naturally tilted his head to the side. Casper smiled, leaned forward as he whispered, "I'm not a vampire."

A flush spread across Roman's face and neck. "I didn't... That's not what I was doing." Even though he felt like an idiot, it was worth it. Casper was smiling wider than he had ever seen before. It was Casper's birthday, and he wanted him to enjoy it. His anxiety could wait until tomorrow. Tonight, he was going to make his boyfriend happy.

Roman slipped a finger in Casper's waistband and tugged him impossibly closer, his head tilted back just slightly. Words failed him; he couldn't think of anything to say. Instead, he used his body. With his free hand, he tugged on the back of Casper's neck; their lips brushed. Roman slipped his tongue out, touching Casper's lips. Then he pulled back, whispering into Casper's ear.

"Why don't we pretend I don't have a boyfriend tonight?"

The bar wasn't far from the dorm, and Casper kept the fire burning. The slight haze of alcohol finally allowed Roman to relax, to welcome each kiss and touch with his own fervent touches and kisses.

Casper dropped him onto his bed, then tugged off his shirt. Casper's broad shoulders and toned physique were on full display. Roman's eyes trailed down Casper's body, down the happy trail as he unbuttoned his jeans. Abandoning them, he leaned over the bed and started working on Roman's shorts. Roman leaned back on his elbows. Who knew the act of undressing could be so hot? Casper was swift in his moments, never hesitating. Roman swallowed the swirling thought of how much experience Casper had.

"Are you sure you want to do this?" Casper asked, kissing up his neck.

"Yes," Roman said breathlessly. He wanted it, he wanted another connection to Casper. He wanted what Joss constantly sought out. What other people thought was so important in relationships, he wanted to do this. Demi and Casper had given him a quick prepping lesson before they started drinking, now he was ready.

Roman leaned back on his elbows, his legs bent, watching Casper slip a slick finger in his ass. Roman stiffened at the intrusion. "We can stop," Casper offered.

Roman shook his head, took a deep breath and relaxed his body. He tipped his head back toward the ceiling.

Casper pumped his dick in unison with his finger. All thoughts became white noise. Casper's encouraging words made his insides squirm. Roman lost count of the time and the number of fingers Casper had inside of him. He let Casper lift his legs and then his dick replaced his fingers.

"Fuck," Roman swore. The difference was noticeable.

"I'm going to go slow. Tell me no or to stop if it's too much."

"I'm okay, just surprising," Roman muttered.

He grabbed onto Casper's arms. Leaning forward, he kissed Casper, whispering against his lips, "I want this. I want you." In a way he did, it might not be the normal desire, but he wanted him.

"I want you so fucking much," Casper admitted. Casper pushed his hips forward, burying himself inside. Roman slipped his tongue in Casper's mouth as he thrusted forward. Casper's pace was slow and steady. His touches gentle and searing. They went round after round. Until Roman woke up to his alarm blaring at him to get ready or miss his flight.

22: Spring Break

The team talked about getting out of the snow and to the warm beaches of Florida. Unfortunately, Florida was where everyone went on spring break, and that was the last thing he wanted to do. He hid in his room from Lara's incessant pushing that he should join them.

"We should do something, go somewhere," Demi said. "The weather should be good near the end of March, we could—"

Roman cut off Demi's excited rambling. "Spring break starts on the ninth for me."

"Uh? Oh. Shit."

Casper took over the conversation. "How about we visit each other? You come here on your break, and we'll go there on ours."

Roman glanced at his tiny room. "I don't know if we'll fit." One night or even two, they could deal with, but a whole week would be grueling.

"I'll rent us a place close to campus. You can stay with us and stay in our dorm when you visit here."

There was no rule they had to stay in the dorms. Everyone did because it was free with their scholarships, who wanted to waste money on an apartment when their dorms were free?

"Okay, let's do it," Roman agreed.

He still had classes, but he would be able to see them every day for an entire week. He thought of the places he accumulated on his list that he wanted to show them now that he had explored the area. His excitement dimmed as the days dragged on. Snow continued to fall and spring break was like a far-off dream.

Roman was packed a week before his departure day, arrived an extra forty minutes early to the airport and landed on time in Georgia. Joss and TJ picked him up, since Casper and Demi were both in class when his flight landed on Thursday afternoon.

"Thanks for picking me up," Roman said as he slid into the back seat, setting his duffle bag on his lap.

Joss twisted around in the passenger seat. "No problem, you hungry?"

"I'm okay."

"Are you going to hang out with me, or are you going to run to your *boyfriends*?" Boyfriends was said mockingly.

Roman rolled his eyes. "I don't know, but every time I see you, you're with your *boyfriend*. I'd ask him to loosen the leash, but you might run away."

TJ snorted, and Joss reached his arm back to slap his leg. Roman dodged, and for a moment, it was high school all over again.

"Also, if he had a car why did you say you would use Casper's?"

"For fun. They say dumb shit all the time to me, Demi does at least."

He wasn't sure he quite understood Joss and Demi's weird friendship.

Roman took his bag with him into TJ's dorm, setting it on the side of the couch. He had returned the borrowed key, so he had to wait for Casper and Demi to come home to unlock the door.

"Wanna play a game?" Joss asked.

Roman nodded. "Do you have a key to the dorm?"

"What dorm? Oh, duh. Yeah, do you want to use it?"

He couldn't believe he forgot that it was Joss's dorm room too. "I'll drop my bag off, you pick a game." Roman caught the tossed keys.

Roman shuffled through the keys till he found the right one, opening the door he hesitated to step inside. As soon as he did, he smelled cookies. Dropping his bag near the shoe rack by the door he stepped into the kitchen where two containers were filled with cookies.

He tugged his phone out of his back pocket.

Roman

Can I have a cookie?

Demi

> You can have 2, but Joss can't have even a
> crumb.

Roman grinned, shaking his head. He took one cookie and finished it before opening TJ's door. It melted in his mouth with an orange flavor.

"What are you eating?" Joss asked.

"Nothing."

"Liar, he made something, didn't he?"

Roman shook his head, but couldn't stop smiling.

Joss tossed the controller to the side and wrestled Roman to the ground. Roman fought back and memories of when they used to wrestle as kids filled him with a happy nostalgia.

On Friday, while Casper and Demi were in class, Roman signed up for the public access time in the hot shop. He worked like it was a job. Halfway through his time, Gwen offered her help.

"Sure, I'm sculpting this one. I have two others in the annealer."

"Wow, you work fast."

He half shrugged. "It's easier when I know what I want to work on."

The conversation dimmed and died as they worked. He rolled, blew and pulled at the molten glass. It shaped under his hands. When he finished one piece, he immediately worked on the next, until his time was up.

He placed the last piece in the annealer. "Thanks, Gwen!" he called out, wiping the sweat from his face.

"You're welcome," she yelled back from the office.

The cool wind chilled his heated skin. He shivered and made a mental note to bring a sweatshirt next time.

On his walk back to the dorm, a piece of paper slapped his face. He paused, grabbed it, and searched for the source.

A girl with gold-rimmed glasses tripped, her bag spilled open and papers took off in the wind, and no one stopped to help. Roman chased a few stray papers and runaway lip balm and pens.

"Thank you! I'm kind of a klutz," she said. Her voice was low and sweet.

Roman handed over the gathered items. "It's no problem. Happy to help."

She brushed back a stray piece of hair, shoving everything back in her bag. "Let me buy you some coffee as a thank you."

Roman shook his head. "You don't have to do that."

She waved him off. "It's not a problem, kindness should always be returned."

"Really?" His eyebrows creased together. He wasn't always clear in the art of flirting, but it sounded like she was hitting on him.

"Yeah. Oh! I'm not hitting on you." She pointed at herself. "I'm a lesbian. I just feel like we've met before. I'm Delia." She held out her hand. Her blonde and pink hair wrapped around her face in the wind. She sputtered, wrapped it in a hair tie, and gave him a wry smile. "I'm a bit of a mess today."

"Roman, I don't really know the campus. I'm just visiting."

She pulled her hand back and snapped her fingers. "Then I know the perfect place! It's just off campus, like a five-minute walk. The place is called The Dragon's Underground. It's a coffee shop during the day and a bar at night; it's really cool. The bar at night has a lot of coffee cocktails, perfect for studying."

She chattered as they walked. He focused on the surroundings so he could find his way back.

"Do you have any hobbies?" she asked.

"I like to make glass, like blowing glass." He clarified to her confused look.

"I've always thought it was really cool. I thought about taking an introduction class for it, you know where you spend like a few hours doing it? I don't really want to do it alone."

"I'm doing it for fun while I'm visiting. If you're free, you could join me." Without the possibility of thinking he was flirting, it was easy to invite her to hangout.

"Really? That would be awesome!" She quietly clapped her hands excitedly.

Roman walked next to Delia, the sidewalks were busy with the traffic of students and residents coming and going. Delia pointed at a while sign with bold brown letters *The Dragon's underground* written on it. There were a few round white tables with latticed white chairs filled with people. They stood in a line that reached the door. Roman glanced around at the artwork for sale on the walls, a display sign said they were local artists. Each held a different style and composition. Some were bold with wide strokes and bright colors. Others were detailed pen drawings devoid of color. For one second, he could imagine one of his drawings on the wall. It wasn't just drawings though, there were glass and clay sculptures. Shelves with painted mugs, bowls and plates for sale that were also made from students of the college.

There were traces of the bar, like the lights that were turned off. He imagined a soft lighting in the bar different from the sunshine shining in through the front windows and open glass door. The menu was electronic, Delia explained that the drinks changed when the bar opened. There were a few options for people to add a shot of Baileys or Kahlua into their morning coffee. Today's special was a lavender iced latte, and tonight's special was a caffeinated old fashioned, with a coffee infused bourbon.

Roman got a hot chocolate, he hadn't been able to stomach coffee so he never ordered it. The hot chocolate tasted decadent, it was full of spices and flavor. It was the best hot chocolate he'd ever had. He got lost in the atmosphere until two texts brought him back.

Casper

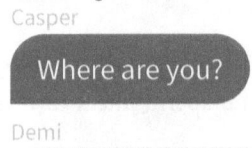

Where are you?

Demi

I thought you were going to beat us to the dorm?

"Oh shit, I have to go. I'm sorry." Roman stood up, starting to leave.

"It's okay, text me, I'm free all day tomorrow."

He paused, turned around, and asked, "Do you really want to try making glass?"

"Absolutely! I'm also serious about texting me about it."

"Alright, I will."

"See you tomorrow."

"Bye." He waved, threw away his empty cup and jogged back to the dorm.

The next day, Roman did as promised and texted Delia. He waited outside of the building for her, kicking a few stray rocks since he arrived early.

"Roman!" she called out, waving her arms. Today she didn't bring a bag with her, and she wore a tight yellow T-shirt, jeans, and sneakers. She had tied her blonde and pink streaked hair up into a neat bun on the top of her head.

"You made it," he said.

"As promised and dressed as you asked." She turned to the door. "So this is it?"

"This is it." Roman opened the door, allowing her to go first. "You have to wear the right clothes or it's a safety issue," he muttered. He knew she knew about it because he added it in his text.

She took a few steps in and stopped. "It's hot."

Roman chuckled behind her.

"Roman?" Gwen called out, her head poking out of the doorway. "Uh. Hi? Did you sign up for a lesson?" Gwen stepped out of the office.

"No, she's with me. I'm going to help her with a project today." He could check on his projects and fix something if it didn't turn out how he wanted it. "Do you want to help us? You're probably a better teacher than me."

"Oh, you didn't tell me you had a girlfriend." Gwen frowned.

"Because I don't. This is Delia, just a friend. I don't think my boyfriends wouldn't like me having a girlfriend, but I also haven't asked either."

Her mouth dropped into an "O" as she took in the information. "Oh, oh okay. Right. Okay. Um, hi, I'm Gwen."

"Delia, nice to meet you." Delia tilted her head and her eyes traveled every inch of Gwen's body. "You're beautiful."

"Thank you? Um, you too. Beautiful, I mean. So, uh, let's go over the basics, yeah?"

Roman bit his lip. He wondered if he had been around too many people that seemed smooth, that Gwen's awkward responses were cute. Similar to a puppy who was just learning how to run.

"So you're dressed good, well, um appropriately," Gwen stuttered out.

"Thanks," Delia said.

"Uh, so we can start with the basics or um, what do you want to make?"

"I'm here to learn, you tell me what to make, I'm pretty easy," Delia said, tilting her head with a sly smile.

Roman turned away from their interactions, realizing how ridiculous it had been to think Delia was flirting with him. With neither of them paying attention, he focused on filling a box with the work he had already completed. He called out with a goodbye and only received mirrored waves of acknowledgement. He figured Delia could have his time slot for the day. Since he already paid and everything he already made came out perfect, so he didn't need to redo anything.

When he got back to the dorm, he carefully set each piece on the coffee table, lining them up, before placing them on the shelf above the TV. He was curious how long it would take them to notice the new items.

Joining the glass orbs, was a white plate with light brown waffles topped with melted butter for Demi. For Casper he made a set of old looking books. And the last thing he made was a white ghost and a black demon pressed together. If pulled apart they could become single statutes, when placed together they fit seamlessly.

An hour later, Casper and Demi walked in the door, Roman sat up eager to get their reactions. They kicked off their shoes, Demi complained about classes and Casper paused as he stared at the shelf, glanced at Roman and stepped closer to get a better look.

"What? Is there a spider? If there's a spider I swear—wait, what are those?" Demi clambered next to Casper. "Oh shit, that's—fuck, is that for us?"

"No, it's actually for Joss. I just put it up there so they didn't break."

"Oh." Demi's shoulders sagged. "Well, they're fucking cool."

"I'm glad you like them. I lied, they are for you guys."

"Fuck yeah!"

Roman grinned and welcomed the pile on from Casper and Demi after they examined and took several pictures of their new treasures.

Roman twitched with awkward energy walking into the Dragons' practice arena, like a child going to work with a parent. It was different when they were there alone, now the whole team was there. He expected to watch them have a grueling practice. Instead, he saw Meena and Keira fake shooting each other with laser tag guns. They both had green paint swiped across their cheeks as if ready for battle.

"It's laser tag day!" Meena yelled, pointing the gun into the air.

"What's laser tag day?" Roman asked, turning to Casper and Demi.

"Fuck," Casper muttered. He turned, trying to leave. Demi yanked him back.

Demi chuckled. "Instead of practice, we're playing laser tag."

"Oh." That sounded fun, though Casper didn't look happy about it.

"We got one for Roman too," Keira announced.

"Uh, thanks?"

"This is a new development this year, Sam suggested it. She said her team did it a lot her senior year of high school and we'll finally have even teams."

Meena snorted. "Ha, it's always been even, having Ghost on your team isn't really an asset."

The rest of the team shuffled in, in intervals. Keira used an app to split everyone into two teams. Roman was on the blue team with Casper, while Demi was on the red team with Joss.

Other than a few casual hellos, he hadn't spent much time with the rest of the Dragons. He only knew them by Demi's gossip. Meena and Sam were hooking up but not in a relationship. Keira had a boyfriend who lived out of state and they were secretly planning on eloping in the fall. Ali was thinking of transferring to the Foxes next year. Roman didn't care for gossip, but he was interested because Demi had shared it with him.

Keira clapped her hands, gaining everyone's attention. "Alright, everyone suit up, let's get this game started."

Roman followed Casper to grab a blue vest, he and TJ grabbed one at the same time. Roman let go, taking the next one in line. He tugged on the vest and looked at the gun attached, his name for the game flashed on the small screen, *SpicyGoat*.

Keira's voice was clear when she spoke. "Everyone, come give me your name so I can put it in the system. After you give me your name, go get in position. Blue is on the row side, red in on the angled side."

The lights in the building shut off. Faint light came off of the bunkers from glow sticks and wireless tap lights that were covered in colored paper in a poor imitation of LED lights. The team targets and vests lit up, marking the start of the game.

Roman moved carefully and quietly, he could hear other people shooting erratically. Some of the vests flashed and low laser sounds went off with every hit, Roman was able to use that to pinpoint where opponents were.

He couldn't stop a smile rising on his face. When he found Demi, he didn't hesitate to shoot him, he snuck away before Demi could retaliate. He slipped behind a bunker and ran into TJ.

"Sorry," Roman whispered.

TJ gave a short hum in response continuing past Roman and running right into Demi.

"Fuck," TJ swore as his vest lit up.

Roman quickened his pace, glad that there was no friendly fire, otherwise he was sure TJ would come after him for not warning him about Demi.

After thirty minutes all of their vests lit up and vibrated signaling the end of the game. It took a few minutes before the lights came on, Roman squinted and blinked against the bright onslaught.

"Gather up!" Keira called out. "The results are in."

Demi and Casper came to either side of him as they joined the others in grouping up around Keira.

Keira clapped her hands. "Blue team wins! First place goes to Oak and last place is Gh—uh, Casper."

"Fuck yeah!" Oak exclaimed, her brown eyes lit up with joy. She waved her toned arms in a victory dance. She whipped her head around, and if it hadn't been shaved, her hair might have had the dramatic impact she was aiming for.

"I fucking hate laser tag," Casper muttered.

Keira passed around a printed sheet showing everyone's score. She also had it on her phone, if they wanted it sent to them. Roman scanned the list and found his name in fourth place, just above TJ. Demi was in second place and Joss was in tenth.

On Sunday, they stayed in lounging in the living room with a movie as background. They didn't need to always do something for him to enjoy their company. Seconds, minutes, hours passed by and he loved every single one of them.

"Can we practice?" he asked, sitting up straight.

Demi groaned. "Ugh more practice. You're lucky I love you otherwise I would say no."

"You love me?" When was the last time he heard someone say they loved him? He couldn't remember. His fingers trembled and his nerves twisted.

"Of course I do." Demi stared at him, there was no trace of teasing in his voice or face.

He admired Demi's straightforward confidence. He tried to open his mouth for a response, but it all came out a stuttered mess.

"I know. I love you too," Casper said.

Roman's mind was a tangle of thoughts and pockets of emptiness. He tried to take a second to compose himself but it was futile. "I—I love you too."

"Should we use pet names?" Demi asked.

Roman didn't respond, ducking his head. He was grateful for the change of topic. Like Joss had said before, he needed five to seven business days to process the confession.

At his request they took him to The Oven to practice. Roman closed his eyes, taking a deep breath, focused his mind and opened them. He made his way toward Demi, weaving through the bunkers. Casper's uniform hung slightly loose from his body. It felt strange, but good. He enjoyed wearing their clothes. He never wanted to admit to his stolen pile of shirts. If he stole the uniform, it would be too noticeable. Roman hid behind a bunker, shifted, pulled back the string and revealed himself as he shot the arrow. He watched Demi bat it away like it was a one-winged fly.

"Gotta try harder than that, darling," Demi called out. He could hear the smile in his voice.

Roman's fingers tingled. Even if it was to tease him. The implication was that he was valued and cared for. It took him longer than he would admit to focus back on scoring against Demi.

Casper took advantage of his absentmindedness to steal a kiss from his cheek before slipping away behind a bunker. They weren't wearing helmets because Roman wasn't shooting at Casper, and Casper's aim was so good he would never hit his head.

Demi was half-decked out in gear. He wore his helmet and arm pad to block the arrows, but otherwise he wore a black T-shirt and dark green shorts. Roman refocused. He wanted to move here. He wanted to be with them all the time. Practicing with them helped him ignore the distractions and work on his approach to the blockers' box.

It was in Demi's favor only having one person to block against, but it was really for Roman to feel the pressure. When they played games against each other, Roman always avoided shooting against Demi.

Roman stood on top of a bunker, his arrow pointed at the target Demi protected. Casper hit his lower back, but he ignored it. Demi was ready. Roman shifted and shot and hit the center of the right target. Demi protecting all three targets was the only way Roman could get a bullseye against him.

Demi hadn't moved from his place protecting the center target, instead, he tilted his head in acknowledgement.

He flipped off of the bunker, something he normally wouldn't do in a game or practice, especially at practice, the coaches hated show-offs, but he was excited. He ran for the targets, an arrow notched. Aiming toward the left one and watched Demi shift, ready to shuffle to block his arrows, an arrow hit the back of Roman's left shoulder. Changing his angle he quickly fired off a shot on the right target. Demi was quick, but didn't reach Roman's arrow that slapped the edge of the target. After shooting his last arrow, he looked down at the uniform. It looked as if he had laid on a pile of powdered donuts.

"Good aim, and you dodged and ignored most of my hits," Casper commented.

"Your footwork needs improvement," Demi said, tugging off his helmet. "Your body language is better than it was, but I still know where you're going to shoot."

This is what he needed. The Capybaras believed in improving individually; that the team was better when the individual was great. Roman thought he could thrive in that kind of environment since he was introverted, but instead he struggled. He enjoyed working with Casper and Demi, intensifying his desire to transfer. He took every piece of advice, like it was a bar of gold.

An entire week flashed by, spending time in the hot shop, hanging out with Joss. The best part of it was feeling like he was actually a part of Casper and Demi's lives. Seeing them come home for class, seeing them leave for class. Being a part of their dinners, watching them practice. He didn't want to go back to Pennsylvania. He wanted to be here, where life was vibrant and he didn't feel so alone. Where he didn't struggle to be friends with the team, where he wanted to transfer, he wanted to play for Port Vista. Transferring would mean the coaches had to accept him, had to think he was worthy of joining the team. He would make them see he was worthy.

Practice arrived on time, the Monday after spring break ended. Determination drove his focus, he was going to show the coaches that he could play, that he could win. They ran through drills that ended with a scrimmage.

"Those extra practices have been helping. Keep up the good work, Wade," Coach Greer told him.

"Thanks, Coach." The best thing the extra practice had done was tone his muscles and build his endurance. He owed all the praise to Casper and Demi for helping him.

The days dragged on as if purposely teasing him. Seconds were like minutes and minutes became days and days were like weeks and that single week felt like a year.

23: Breaking Springs

Roman checked his phone for the fifth time in twenty minutes. There was only ten minutes of class left and three hours until Demi and Casper's flight should be landing. They still had practice Saturday so they had to fly in on Sunday.

Casper had already sent the information about the house and told him he could go there first if he wanted. Demi sent him a shopping list. Roman wanted everything to be perfect, so he decided to shop, then they could relax when they got there. They always did so much for him when he visited them, he wanted to pay that back even it was just going grocery shopping.

Roman looked through the list, making sure he got every item and nothing was missing. He threw in a few things that looked good as he passed by, a few different kinds of snacks and drinks. Demi had added a few liquors, Roman perused through the aisles not sure which shelves they would be on. The aisles were full of college kids, several of them grabbing handles off of the bottom shelf. Roman checked, but the ones Demi texted him weren't there.

After searching a few more aisles, he finally found one. Like it was an adult scavenger hunt. There were so many different types and flavors. It opened a whole new world, most of the time he just drank what was provided, he never looked any deeper at his options.

After gathering everything on the list, he hired a car. The house was hidden down a long driveway obscured by trees. It was only a fifteen-minute walk to the closest part of campus.

"I can take the bus," Roman offered.

"Don't worry about it. I'll drive you," Demi said.

"If you're sure."

"A thousand percent."

The house had more bedrooms than they needed. It was a two-story half brick house. White panels and wood weaved through the entire house, with a mix of light and dark wood. He dropped his bags in the primary bedroom. In the bathroom was a large jet tub and a glass-door shower spacious enough for four people.

All the cold groceries were placed in the fridge, and he left the rest on the kitchen table for Demi to go through. Roman wandered around the house a few times, not really sure what to do. He was restless and finally forced himself to sit and turn on the TV, so he didn't seem weird by standing at the front door like a lovesick puppy. Roman channel surfed before leaving it on a nature documentary. He glanced at his phone. No new messages.

He ran a hand through his hair. It was getting long, but he hadn't bothered trying to find someone to cut it. When working out or practicing, he wore a headband to hold it back. Half of his wardrobe was Capybara branded clothes. If he transferred, his wardrobe would change from pink to green. Right now, it was easier than going shopping. It also gave him a reason to wear so much pink, even if he looked like he was going to a kid's princess party all the time.

Tugging on a plush sage green throw blanket, he draped it over his legs, cushioning his head on a pillow.

Roman startled awake to the sound of the front door opening. He sat up, turning around to the noise.

"Honey, we're home," Demi called out. "There you are."

Roman stood up, trying to dispel the mental fog. Demi wrapped his arms around him and Roman hugged him back as he saw Casper walk in the door with their bags.

"I went shopping," Roman said. Demi released him and Casper took his place.

"If you're still tired, you can keep napping. You look like you just woke up."

"Ah, I'm okay. Do you want to see the house?"

"Sure."

He threw the fallen blanket back on the couch and led Casper like he was a realtor. Grocery bags crinkled, and the fridge door opened and shut. The sounds muffled the further in the house they went until it was just their breathing and footsteps pattering across the floor.

Casper dropped the bags at the end of the bed, pulling Roman into another hug. His arms tightened. Roman put his hands on Casper's hips. Casper kissed his head, then his ear, cheek and nose before lastly kissing his lips. Roman smiled into the kiss, his fingers squeezing Casper.

The kiss turned feverish and hasty. Casper's fingers slipped under Roman's shirt. Roman never thought about fingers before being with Casper and Demi. He loved their fingers. Casper's were calloused, gentle and teasing. The taller man pulled back, pressing their foreheads together.

"I missed you," Casper whispered.

"I missed you too."

He hated being away from them, but the idea of being with them every day was like a fantasy he would never be able to achieve. He never felt good enough, he was always lacking something, his parents thought so, his coaches thought so and sooner or later Casper and Demi would also think so. But he would enjoy every second he had, while he had it.

Demi made them spaghetti for dinner, showered, and the rest of the time they hung out in the master bedroom, letting the day slip by them.

Roman pressed into the tattoo on Casper's chest as they lay in bed. "Why a slow loris?"

"Most people don't know what it is."

"I watch a lot of nature documentaries," Roman murmured, still admiring the realistic fine line tattoo.

"It's my favorite animal." Casper poked his forehead. "I wanted a tattoo, but I didn't know what to get so I got something that I liked."

"It was his last fuck you to his parents," Demi added, reclining against his raised arm while he searched for something to watch.

Casper nudged Demi with his knee. "They hate tattoos. It was a stupid reason to get one, but I like it."

"Should I get one?" Roman didn't have a reason to get one, but he also didn't have a reason not to.

"If you want one, then do it."

Demi sat up, his hand on Casper's knee as he leaned over him to talk to Roman. "We should get matching ones!" He settled down again at Roman's laugh.

"Maybe we should," Roman whispered. He slid over Casper so he could lay in the middle. His favorite place to be.

Roman tried to memorize every detail, like the small freckle on Casper's right ear just above his earlobe. Specks of gold in Demi's dark brown eyes and specks of darkness in Casper's light brown eyes. The way Casper's jaw clenched and his fingers flexed when he tried not to laugh or smile in public or his eyes crinkling just slightly to show he was happy without any large emotion. Demi looked like an open book, but sometimes he was as closed off as Casper, they just presented it in opposite manners. He had watched Demi's smile get wider at a few of Joss's comments, but it never showed in his eyes. He wanted to memorize the tiniest of things, like the small thin white scars on Demi's fingers.

"I wasn't always a professional chef," Demi told him as Roman twisted his fingers.

They fell asleep with the TV on low to an old sitcom, legs tangled under the covers.

The next morning started early, Demi made waffles, eggs and sausage before dropping him off as close as he could get to his morning class. His leg shook all throughout class, he couldn't wait to get classes and practice over with so he could get back to them. His impatience played in his favor at practice during the scrimmage when he shot all of his arrows, gaining several points. He didn't even look at the team board to see if he moved places before he rushed out to meet up with Demi and Casper, who were waiting in the car for him.

They got dinner on the way and started breaking into the alcohol. They started off strong with a shot and then made a mixed drink with vodka and juice.

A baking show was on the TV as they relaxed. Casper was reading, and Demi was typing away on his phone. Some kind of drama was brewing with his teammates.

"Can you teach me how to give a blow job?" Roman asked. He finished his mixed drink, setting it on the coffee table.

Demi's eyes opened wide and then creased into crescents. "Fuck yes I can." He nudged Roman's side. "Right now?"

"You don't want to?" Roman asked. Joss had been the one to tell him to ask. Joss had too much advice on his sex life. He knew it was out of worry for him. Just because he was asexual didn't mean he couldn't be sexual. The alcohol helped, it boosted his confidence and gave him the bit of desire he needed. He didn't care if the desire was manufactured, his feelings weren't. He knew he didn't have to do anything. He wanted to. To show them he loved them. Sex was just exercise with partners and exercise was one thing he knew he was good at.

Demi paused. "No, no, now is good." He pulled Roman to stand up, moved the coffee table back, and steered him to stand in front of Casper, who hadn't lifted his head from his book. Noticing the new shadows, his head tilted up.

"What?"

Demi smiled mischievously, causing Casper's eyes to narrow. "Roman's going to give you a blow job."

Roman's head bobbed several times, his eyes alight with excitement.

"Why are you here, then?" Casper asked provocatively.

Demi chuckled. "I'm going to teach him how to give a very good blow job."

"Is that right?"

"Of course, besides, you're probably getting hard just from thinking about the possibility, right?"

Casper grinned with a shrug. "Who am I to turn down a blowjob?"

Demi lightly pressed on Roman's shoulders guiding him to his knees. The carpet cushioned his knees, and he adjusted to make the position more comfortable.

"Don't mind us, you keep reading," Demi told him.

"Fine, I will."

Demi leaned down, whispering in Roman's ear. "First, you want to tease a bit." Demi nodded his head towards Casper, where Roman could see his Adam's apple shifting. Demi guided Roman's hands over Casper's muscled thighs. The book in Casper's hands trembled. Roman grinned, *teasing is pretty fun.*

He watched Casper's bulge grow, it was impossible to hide when he was only wearing a pair of black briefs. His hands slid over his thighs, closer and closer before he pulled back. He hadn't heard any pages being flipped. Casper was a quick reader and should have already changed the page.

Casper's dick moved, as if urging him to do something.

"Go ahead," Demi said.

He swallowed the gathering salvia in his mouth and slipped his fingers in the fly and freed Casper's penis from the confines of the briefs. Roman wasn't a stranger to a penis, and he wasn't a stranger to this penis. But it was a little different when it was this close to his face. He licked his lips, tilting his head up at Demi for another direction.

"Lick it," Demi instructed.

Roman was a marionette. He licked across the head of Casper's penis, earning a sharp inhale of breath from Casper. He licked a stripe from the base to the tip, circling his tongue around the tip before closing his lips around it, sinking down then pulling back up, each time going further. The velvet dick throbbed in his mouth, spurring him to go faster and deeper, Demi's encouraging words and small tips tickled his ears.

"Fuck, Fuck, Ro—" It was his only warning before his mouth was filled with salty semen. He coughed and choked, his eyes watering as he pulled back and covered his mouth.

"Beautiful." Demi kissed his temple. "Let's get you some water and maybe a toothbrush."

Twenty minutes later, they moved to the bedroom and to the bed. Roman lay on his back, head resting on the edge, licking his lips. Demi knelt in front of him, teasing his sides with his hands, while Casper stood before him, holding Roman's face gently between his hands.

"We can stop at any time or change positions." Casper's voice was low and gentle.

"I know," Roman said. Roman wasn't interested in sex to have sex. He could never have the numbers of partners Joss had. But he liked the way it felt, he probably wouldn't seek it out on his own, but he would do it with Casper and Demi. He loved the attention they gave him, the way they connected together, he wanted everything they offered.

Roman was already prepped when Demi lifted his legs and slipped his dick between his ass cheeks. Roman opened his mouth giving Casper access. Casper's dick was longer, but Demi's was thicker. Demi started slow, an unusual pace for him, pushing Roman toward Casper.

Roman got lost in the feeling of being filled and so intertwined like marbling glass, the only way to separate them was to shatter them. He slowly came back to himself and sucked hard on Casper's dick.

"Fuck," Casper swore. Roman fought a grin.

Demi's pace quickened, his hands tightly gripped Roman's hips. Roman was sure he would have bruises tomorrow. Casper's dick slammed into his throat as they pounded into him from both ends. Roman jolted when Demi grabbed his penis.

Demi chuckled. "So fucking hot."

"If you cum first you lose," Casper teased.

"Fuck. Fuck that, whoever cums first, wins."

Hearing his words, Roman quit fighting against his orgasm.

Roman woke up surrounded in warmth, wrapped between strong limbs. To some it may have been a suffocating heat, but he felt safe.

They got into a rhythm with his schedule and sex. Sometimes he would wake up to a blow job and sometimes he went to bed with one. Between the various positions, his body contorted in ways he never knew possible.

The days went by too quickly for him to grasp. Roman went back to his dorm, boneless and more knowledgeable about the practical use of sex positions that Joss had told him stories of. It was interesting to be inside of the story, instead of as an outsider listening in. Later that night, his eyes opened with the fear that the owners had put secret cameras around the house.

24: PLAYOFFS

Starting in April, a new coach joined them for an hour every day at practice. He was introduced as Parker Woods, a parkour instructor.

"Yes, I know. Let's hear all the jokes about how my name is Parker and I'm a parkour instructor."

The team laughed and quiet chatter filled the area.

"Are we supposed to jump between the bunkers?" Lara asked.

The teacher looked around. "It's not impossible, but I'm here to teach you to gain balance on the bunkers and control over your footing. I am also here to help you learn how to fall off of the bunkers safely."

Not every runner was confident climbing, shooting and jumping off of the bunkers. A lot of them actually stayed on the ground, only using the bunkers as a way to hide and sneak around. Some players didn't think using the bunkers for climbing as worth it. If you got hurt and couldn't play anymore, your scholarship disappeared with it. Most players waited until the end of their senior year to take more risks in the playoffs.

Roman paid attention to the instructions and copied the moves as closely as he could. He stood still as the instructor stood him up straight and held his waist.

"Be careful of how you turn when rolling into the fall. You don't want to pull a muscle."

Roman nodded, and the instructor let go and stepped back. Roman took a few seconds to refocus and then rolled into a fall.

"Great," the instructor called out. Roman got into line and listened to the girls gush over their 'hot' instructor.

"Maybe I should mess up so he can touch me?" Yueying said.

"I might just trip on him and have him catch me," Haijun added.

"That's a good idea."

Roman was dismissed from doing extra practices, because practices became infinitely more difficult.

The weight of being a college evobe player yanked at his ankles and pressed down on his shoulders. They had finished another practice that left him exhausted. His improvement depended on his own abilities, he knew that. They only had two chances in the playoffs. It was a double elimination. The first loss would put them in the losers bracket, and the second would knock them out of the playoffs. He wanted to be worthy of Casper and Demi, he wanted to be worthy of transferring to their school.

Roman dragged himself toward the target range. He tried not to hate evobe or going to practice, but it was getting hard. It wasn't fun anymore; it was work. It was putting everything he had into something that he would never perfect. Evobe was how he could afford college without graduating with debt. If he got denied from Port Vista, he would continue to endure Pennsylvania because he didn't have any other option.

Roman took shot after shot after shot, until the target had a ring of white along the outer edge. A few arrows had strayed off the path, but the circle was nearly complete.

"What are you doing?" He jumped and his arrow fell short dropping to the ground in a pitiful arc.

"Practicing," Roman said, turning to Lara.

Lara wore a dark pink capybara shirt and leggings. "I see that. Why does it look like some weird ritual?"

Roman looked back at the target, it did look a little strange.

"Just practicing my aim."

She shrugged, a smile tugging at her lips. "How about a competition?"

"Doing what?"

"Whatever it is you're doing." Her hand waved toward the target. "Making a donut?"

A competition would add some pressure, but his shoulder might not hold out. "Uh, sure."

"Cool, let's do it around the middle ring though, then you don't have to clean it off and it'll go a bit faster."

"Okay, I just need a drink of water." He went to his bag while she kept talking.

"First one to finish or should we do whoever has the best-looking circle?"

He slipped half a pill into his hand and threw it in his mouth, washing it down with a gulp of water. He wasn't an idiot, if he was going to do something stupid, he would do it smartly. Just enough to take the pain's edge off, not enough to affect his reflexes or impairment. So far it was working. He would never use it in a game. He just needed to make it through practices.

"Both?" he asked.

"Bold, I like it. Deal."

"Are we betting on anything?"

"Nope. Just for bragging rights. Besides, you don't have anything I want." She winked.

"How about lunch?"

"Alright, if you want to take me to lunch so bad, then let's do that. Loser pays for lunch."

Roman rolled his eyes, he just needed some pressure.

The days slipped by and their first official playoffs game of the year started. The Foxes were a team that adapted well to other teams' rhythms, making them a hard team to gain a lead against.

Roman stood at the edge of the field, the crowd was a blur of cheerful static. Players weaved around the field, appearing and disappearing from his view. Three seconds until he substituted for Natya. Two seconds. One second. She passed the outfield line, and he jogged in, nocking an arrow on his bowstring.

Pressed against a bunker on the outer edge, he took a steadying breath, his heart pounding. He raised his bow and released the arrow, pink paint splattered from the tip, scoring his first point of the night against a bright orange uniform.

He quickly moved on, going deeper into the field, weaving through teammates, opponents, and bunkers. He slipped behind a bunker. He could hear another player on the other side. Roman continued so they slipped by each other, passing by bunkers on the outer edge.

Another bright orange opponent entered his view, this time they stood in front of the target, he waited till their attention shifted to Lara on the bunker to his right. Roman took his shot, hitting the five ring. He didn't take the time to celebrate. He pulled back, knowing the other team would track him down. Roman was quick on his feet, shifting back and hiding behind a bunker. He tugged out another arrow, ready to gain more points. His opponents were just colors, he just needed to focus on hitting the moving colors, he took another steadying breath and stepped away from the bunker.

Roman stood under the cold spray of water. They lost. No matter how much he had improved, they still lost. He still wasn't good enough. The Dragons had won their first game, last week. Joss would always be better than him. He wondered if Demi and Casper thought that as well. Joss had time to win them over. Roman was a random guy, in another state that they sometimes enjoyed hanging out with.

His insecurities clung to his skin like stains, no matter how hard he scrubbed they didn't wash away. Roman shut the water off. The water slipped down the drain.

Several texts were waiting for him after he dried off and got dressed. Two from Demi and one from Casper.

Demi

That shot was awesome!

Call us when you're free. XOXO

Casper

Great job! I'm proud of you.

Roman stared at his phone while the rest of the team finished getting dressed and talked about going out to eat and getting drinks. Roman went back to the hotel alone. He settled into his room, wrapping his blanket around his shoulders. He channel surfed, avoiding the call he would inevitably make. They would make him feel better and he wanted to wallow.

It was the first time he was starting and they lost. He groaned, covering his face with a pillow. He worked hard to become a starter but it didn't matter. They still lost. He knew his thoughts and insecurities were stupid and nonsensical. His brain wouldn't shut off just because he knew that. He tried so hard, pushed through the constant pain in his shoulder and they lost.

When his avoidance tactics didn't keep his mind preoccupied long enough, his fingers slipped away from the remote, to his phone and video called Casper. He answered on the third ring, Casper became a blur on the screen as the phone moved, Demi's smiling face appeared.

"You were awesome! You only got hit twice."

Roman shrugged one shoulder. "We still lost."

"The Foxes know how to gain points against blockers. It doesn't mean you weren't great. It's a team sport, losing isn't on you, not after that performance today. You have no idea how many highlight videos have been made of you. You're on everyone's radar and that's not easy to do and you did it with your hard work, unlike Casper whose good looks open every door."

Roman rolled his eyes, Casper had been playing evobe before evobe was a sport.

Demi continued talking when Roman didn't respond. "You should celebrate."

If he wanted to celebrate losing, he would have followed the team. He glanced at the door when someone knocked. Hopping up, careful with the ice on his shoulder, he walked to the door. "Hold on, there's someone at my door."

Roman tugged open the door to Demi and Casper standing on the other side. Roman looked at his phone, but Demi had already hung up, he hadn't even noticed where they were.

"We went to your game, you were awesome. I wish you would get a Tiptap so I could send you all of the videos of people gushing over you."

"No thanks." Roman moved aside to let them into his room. He had already gotten a photogram; he didn't want to get anything else.

"Did you hurt your arm?" Casper asked.

"No, it's just a little overworked." He tossed the ice in the sink by the door. "I don't really need it, just trying to be careful." He threw himself on the bed, ready to bury himself in the blanket again.

"So mopey, I promise you did amazing." Demi tugged on his ankle, yanking him towards the edge of the bed. Roman clung to the sheet. "How about a celebratory blow job?"

Roman let go of the sheets, poking his head out. His sore shoulder instantly forgotten.

Demi grinned down at him. "Want one?"

Roman licked his lips, nodding.

"Are you going to stop moping?"

Roman nodded again. Demi threw aside the blanket and made quick progress with his offer. After five minutes, Roman lay on the bed, sated.

"Hungry?" Casper asked. "Do you want to get takeout or go out?"

"Take out," Roman said. He didn't want to leave the room. Even getting off of the bed felt like too much effort.

Casper smiled at him, then glance back down at his phone. "What kind of food?"

"Anything," he replied.

"So picky, how will we ever choose?" Casper teased.

Roman grinned, the disappointment from losing faded, his insecurities assuaged by their arrival. They still had another game to play, it wasn't the end of their season yet. Except it was the most important game, they would either lose and their season would finish or they would win and continue.

25: WHATEVER IT TAKES TO WIN

After the last game, he was determined to get them their next win. He watched his name rise on the team board. He was so close to victory he could feel it in his bones. They were going to win. This was possibly their last game of the season. He had to prove that he was good enough to transfer to the Dragons. He wanted to play with Casper and Demi, not as opponents, but as teammates. They had won their first game, but lost their second, dropping them into the loser bracket with them.

He held the two pills in his hand; it would be so easy to swallow them down. If he got caught, he would be suspended, or in the worst case, he would be banned from the sport, but if he didn't, he might not be able to shoot. He had tried icing it, heating it, even rubbing an egg on it. Time was running out. He was number four on the team board, a starting player. He couldn't stop now.

He had watched the Dragons play. He felt a little scummy at being a spy; he hadn't shared anything. But he knew how to beat them. He could do it; he just needed the opportunity. He had been careful to only take enough pain medication to numb the pain, but never during a game. But his shoulder was throbbing, making his fingers twitch. He had to make a choice. Gripping the pills tightly, he took a deep breath and grabbed his water.

The coach knocked her clipboard against the locker, gaining everyone's attention. "This is the lineup today for blockers: Addams, Morcilla, and Walz. For the runners: Tate, Wade, Ling, and Lamb."

The rest of the coach's words slipped through his ears, he was starting the game off, this was his chance. Excitement overrode any bit of anxiety.

He stood on the edge of the field, bow lowered at his side, his gaze sweeping across the field in front of him, his right fingers twitched in anticipation. They had to win this game to stay in the Playoffs. If they lost, it would be over. He was glad their helmets hid their faces, he couldn't stop the grin on his face. They were going to win, he knew it.

The whistle blew and Roman rushed onto the field with his fellow runners.

Period 1 20:00 Capybaras: 0 Dragons: 0

Allen: The Capybaras are not playing it safe. They're attacking from the start. It's a good play against the Dragons who take a period to warm up.

Tamara: Galloway has improved in the months leading up to the playoffs, I can't say the same for Talkbot whether the Capybaras can break through or not, we'll find out today.

Tamara: Graves has found his focus again, I was wondering if he would be able to or if he would continue his spiral from last year.

Allen: After what happened, I'm surprised he came back to play for the Dragons. There was a lot of talk that he would transfer to Thunder.

Tamara: There is a lot of speculation about why his shooting declined, injury, mental illness, rebellion, and a transfer. He seems to have beaten those rumors.

Allen: Whatever his reasons are it's not an excuse to play like that. He needed to be taken off the field a lot sooner than he was.

Period 1 4:29 Capybaras: 23 Dragons: 14

Tamara: Only 4 minutes and 30 seconds left of the first period and the Capybaras have a 9-point lead.

Allen: Now a 12-point lead as Wade hits the outer ring of Talkbot's target.

Tamara: They need to replace her with someone else. She gives away points like charity canned fruit. They need to switch her with Alishba Shea. Galloway and Knight have become a solid force, but Talkbot is an unstable brick in the wall.

Allen: Having no one there is better than having her stand there. And the switch is being made as a penalty is called against the Dragons' Barrera for a headshot on the Capybaras' Wade.

Period 2 6:21 Capybaras: 34 Dragons: 35

Tamara: This is the first lead the Dragons have taken this game. They're warmed up now, the Capybaras should get ready.

Allen: The Dragons are excellent at working together and creating plays to maximize their points. The Capybaras focus on individual tactics, it gives them the edge of being hard to predict, but unless they can gather the points, they'll be walking off the field losers.

Period 3 20:00 Capybaras: 38 Dragons: 42

Tamara: It's the beginning of the third period. What changes do you think the Dragons are going to make to gain a strong lead over the Capybaras?

Allen: The Capybaras are not far behind. A couple of shots on a target and they'll catch up. As long as Alishba Shea stays in the block-er box with Galloway and Knight, the Dragons will win tonight.

Tamara: The Dragons are attacking the targets and the Capybaras. Park blocks Barker's arrow. North gets 5 points against Walz.

Allen: Singh scores 3 points against Galloway. Addams blocks Barrera's second shot. Arrows are flying and points are rising. Graves gets a bullseye from Park. Wade gets 3 points from Galloway. Lamb gets 5 points from Knight. Barker and Graves each get 3 points from Addams. Wade gets 5 points from Knight. Lamb gets 1 point from hitting Graves. Graves gets a point from hitting Wade.

Tamara: I can't keep up with the amount of arrows flying. This may be the first time we get to a cease all. To explain what that means, it's when all players on both of the teams have used all of their given arrows and substitutes.

```
Period 3 9:00 Capybaras: 59 Dragons: 66
```

Allen: Wade spun away, Graves misses his shot. It looks like Wade dropped; his helmet is coming off. Did you see what happened?

Tamara: I'm not sure. It happened pretty fast. We'll have to watch the replay.

Roman heard a pop and his knee gave out.

"Fuck fuck fuck," he stuttered out.

He dropped his bow and tugged off his helmet, letting it roll away. The drugs barely numbed any of the pain, he sucked in short breaths as Casper dropped next to him. He tried to ignore everyone staring, to just ignore everything. The sharp stabbing pain was excruciating; it radiated from his knee to his toes and up his waist.

"Is it your ankle or knee?" Casper asked.

"I heard a pop," he gritted out.

Casper made space for the medic, telling him what had happened. The medic moved next to him, covering his knee in ice. "You may have torn your ACL. Let's get him on the stretcher," he called out.

"But the game—" Roman started.

"Sorry, but it's over. This isn't something to play with."

He knew that, he knew what a torn ACL meant. All this time he was so worried about his shoulder and winning the game and in the end it didn't matter. He covered his face with his arm as they carried him off of the field. His lips trembled as tears slid down the side of his face.

It was over, everything was gone in a single second.

The hospital was stark and desolate, they gave him more pain medication. He stared at the ceiling blankly. He knew he wasn't alone, but his body was too heavy, and his mind was hazy.

"We'll lower the dosage," a nurse said.

He rolled his head towards her, Assistant Coach Greer and Doctor Lavoie stood with their arms crossed, frowns on their faces. He just wanted to sleep, but the lights were stabbing his eyes.

"I want to eat a chili cheese dog with mustard," he slurred out. "Can we turn off the sun in here?"

The lights dimmed and his eyes burned a little less.

When he was lucid, Doctor Lavoie explained what happened. "With the degree of tear, you won't be playing next season. You may also need surgery."

He opened his mouth, it was dry, but he didn't dare ask for a cup of water. What had he done?

"That means..."

"You lost your sports scholarship."

"I can't afford to go to school without it."

"There are loans, the manager can help you if you need it or they can speak to your advisor."

Roman shook his head. "What about the dorm?"

"You'll have to move out to allow for the new freshman to move in. I know it seems abrupt and this is a lot."

He scoffed. A lot? This was his entire future crumbling in front of him. The drugs in his system were the only things keeping him in the bed. A part of him wanted to flip the tray table, to shake the coach and ask them how they could be so uncaring that a player they taught just ended their career.

"You have two weeks to move out, there are more scholarships you can apply for and—"

None of the words reached his ears, all he could hear was gurgling water. He was going to have to move home. Transferring to Port Vista was now impossible. No one would accept a broken player.

"You have some friends here who want to see you, but we wanted to talk to you first."

"Can you tell them to wait outside for a little bit longer?"

"Sure." The doctor got up and left, giving a pat to his arm.

Roman's eyes closed, he could barely remember anything he had been told, he just knew everything was gone. The pain killers were wearing off, the nurse would be coming in for a meds soon. He covered his eyes with his hands. It was his fault, he wasn't enjoying evobe anymore, it was some universal justice for not telling the team doctor about his shoulder. What right did he have to be angry? What right did he have to feel frustrated? It was all his fault. This was what he deserved. He would be lucky if Casper and Demi didn't walk in the door and break up with him.

Casper, Demi, Joss, and Lara filed into the room with hesitant expressions.

"These losers decided to follow me," Lara said.

"It's okay," he said, voice low.

Lara dropped to his side, Demi moved around the bed to his left side. Casper stood at the end of the bed while Joss tried pulling Lara off of the bed.

"Move," Joss demanded.

Lara shook him off. "No, fuck off. You're going to hurt him."

"I'm going to hurt him? You're the one crowding him."

Roman forced a smile. Demi squeezed his hand.

"Hey, are you okay?" he asked.

Roman shook his head, picking at the thin white hospital blanket. How could he be okay? Everything he worked for was gone in a single moment. Demi pulled his head to his chest, arms tight around his body.

"Why don't you go grab some food or something," Demi suggested.

Lara pointed at herself.

"Yeah, you and him." Demi lifted his chin, indicating Joss.

"Fine, let's go." Lara pushed Joss who pushed her back as they left.

Casper remained at the end of the bed, like a very good-looking gargoyle.

Roman held his hand out. Casper hesitated then with drooped shoulders, came to his right side.

"I'm sorry," Casper said.

Roman's brows creased. "For what?"

"It's my fault, if I hadn't shot at you, then—"

Roman shook his head. "It could have been anyone and maybe it's a good thing?" He rubbed at his shoulder. "Maybe it's a wake up call."

"Wake up call for what?" Casper asked.

"I—" He swallowed the truth, the truth could die with his evobe career. "I didn't know what I wanted to do in college anyway and I think I know what I want to do instead."

"And what is that?" Casper asked softly.

"I want to make art. I want to start glass blowing again." That was the truth, he had missed it and maybe he would have gone back to it as a hobby instead of a career choice, but if he spent the rest of his life working in the hot shop, he wouldn't complain. Or maybe he was just saying it because he had nothing else he could do, no other option at his disposal. The reality was that he had no idea what he was going to do.

Casper kissed his hand. "I wish you at least threw a pillow or something at me."

"Is it okay that I can't play anymore?"

"What do you mean?"

"I—thought maybe..." Roman pulled his hand away from Casper, clenching it in his lap. "Maybe you would want to break up..."

Casper lifted his chin, Roman looked to the side. "Can you look at me?"

Roman lifted his eyes to meet Casper's. He looked angry.

His voice was steady and calm as he spoke. "Don't say stupid shit like that. I don't care about evobe. I don't care if you play or don't play. Demi could quit today, and I would probably quit with him."

"He's right, I think it's better this way. You can come to all of our games and maybe move to Port Vista..." Demi trailed off, a smile playing on his lips. He was forever hinting, instead of just asking.

They didn't stop liking him because he couldn't play evobe anymore. They didn't just abandon him. Even if he felt useless, all that time he trained to feel like he was worth something, every minute and hour he put into it, had gotten him exactly where he wanted to be. A starting player, he had reached his goal, it was in his grasp and then it all slipped away.

"I hope you're hungry," Joss said, throwing open the room door. Lara followed behind him with two bags stretched full.

He wasn't alone, though. Even if his parents stopped caring about him, as much as he should be used to their silence, to their lack of regard for what he wanted, it didn't stop him from hoping, from wanting them to call. But for the moment, while visiting hours were still going on, he wasn't alone.

26: FINALS

Roman weaved through fellow travelers; he had twenty minutes to get to the other side of the airport, and he was on crutches. He slipped in line for the shuttle, checking the time while they waited. If nothing else delayed him, he would have a few minutes to spare.

Settling against a pole on the bus, he replied to Demi.

Demi

> Are you going to watch the game?

Roman

> I will. I'm sorry I can't see it in person.

Demi

> Not your fault your sister was born this weekend. We'll be together all summer.

Roman

> Best summer ever!

Roman grinned, his body vibrating with anxiety and excitement. He was going to surprise them. He had to go through Natya to get information and a free ticket from TJ, asking Joss would have ruined the surprise. He could never keep a secret, he would probably just brag that he was the one getting his ticket instead of them.

Unfortunately, he couldn't stay long. Sunday afternoon he was flying out to Arizona for his sister's birthday party. His parents wouldn't answer his phone calls, but they mailed his sister's birthday invite. He wasn't sure why he had been invited, but hoped that his parents wanted to see him because they missed him. He didn't join them on her birthday trip last year, so inviting him to her party this year felt strange after all of the silence. He got the latest flight he could on Sunday without missing the party completely.

He got a hotel for two nights in Arizona, but he hadn't bought his ticket home yet, in case his parents wanted him to stay longer. He also didn't expect to stay at their house after hearing about their plans with his room.

Roman dropped into his window seat with a sigh of relief, shoving his bag under the seat in front of him. He folded down the crutches and the flight attendant put them in the compartment above him.

Demi

> Sucks your sister's bday is this weekend.

Roman

> Agreed.

Casper

> I miss your face. I'm sick of dealing with Demi alone.

Demi

> Hey! I'm the fun one. Maybe we'll go on a trip by ourselves.

Casper

> Yeah? On my credit card? I'll just cancel it.

Demi

> That's evil

Casper

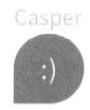

Roman turned his phone on airplane mode and contemplated their offer. He was finally able to see them for an entire summer. He was going to fly to Port Vista after Arizona to finish packing, then spend the summer with them until he moved into an apartment in August.

He shifted against the window, looking out as they pulled away from the airport. His stomach dropped as the plane took off. He had never been afraid of flying, but it was one of the ways he didn't want to die. He would rather be attacked by a horde of zombies. Something about dropping out of the sky and crashing into the ground didn't appeal to him.

The plane landed safely in Washington. Taking his phone off airplane mode, text messages from Casper and Demi popped upon one after the other. With no checked bags, he walked off of the plane and out of the airport. The air was humid and sunshine blinded him as a light wind greeted him. He leaned on his crutches as he found his hired car.

The only flaw to his plan was that he had no idea what room they were in or if they were even at the hotel. He at least knew what hotel they were at, in the lobby he called Demi. Knowing he would get more information from him than Casper.

"Roman, you scared me, you didn't text back."

"Sorry, I took a nap so I missed your texts."

"Naps are good."

"What are you guys up to?"

Demi sighed dramatically. "Hanging out at the hotel until we head out for dinner."

"Ah, I stayed on the fifth-floor last time we played in Washington." Roman bit his thumb near his nail, it wasn't as smooth as he hoped. Demi knew what floor he was on last time, because they were on the floor below him.

Demi either didn't realize the conversation was strange or didn't care. "We're on the seventh floor we got a corner room so we can see more of the sunset, the windows meet in the corner, so it's pretty cool," Demi said, sighing loudly. "Too bad you're not here, you could be enjoying it with us."

Roman headed to the elevator, with a smile. The hotel was setup so he had two options for which room they were in.

"I think odd room numbers are lucky."

"Shit. Cas we gotta switch rooms, we need an odd room. Maybe then someone's birthday will be canceled, and he can watch us win tomorrow."

Roman bit at his lips trying not to look like a grinning idiot, he loved that Demi was predictable enough to tell him where he was.

"We're not switching rooms," Casper's voice was clear through the phone.

Roman stepped out of the elevator, heading west. He stopped at the last door in the hallway on the left, his heart pounding in his chest. Casper and Demi continued to bicker through the phone, though it was muffled, he could hear them through the door. Knowing he had the right door gave him the confidence to knock. He hung up the phone when he heard Demi question who was knocking.

The door opened and Demi froze for less than a second before launching at Roman, wrapping his arms around him and spinning him around. The crutches falling to a clatter on the ground.

"You precious beautiful little sneak."

"Who?" Casper asked.

Demi set him down and was yanked away by Casper who pulled him in, Casper kissed his forehead several times. He was tugged into their room. Roman dropped his bag on the floor, just past the door. Demi slipped his arms around his waist, sandwiching him in. They were careful with his knee as they brought him toward the king-sized bed. They set him in the middle of it. Demi carefully tugged off his shoes and joined him on the bed. He was cautious as crept over his left side and Casper pressed into his neck.

"We're having dinner with Casper's parents tonight. You should join us."

Roman shook his head. "I don't want to intrude. I can just get some takeout or hangout with Joss."

After twenty minutes they broke apart, but stayed close. Roman tugged his phone out from here where it had slid under him.

Roman

Want to meet up for dinner?

Joss

?? Wrong person? Are you in Washington?

Roman

I'm in Washington, surprise.

Joss

You little shit! Where are you?

Roman

Hanging out in Casper and Demi's room.

Joss

Of course those fuckers didn't tell me anything.

Roman didn't burst Joss's bubble thinking this surprise was for him.

Joss

I thought you were heading home. It's the little demon's birthday, right?

Demi held out the remote, switching through channels creating a low murmur in the background.

Ten minutes before Roman left for Joss's room, Demi took selfies before and after they dressed up for dinner. If there was one thing he could always count on Demi to do, it was take photos.

"If I knew you were coming, I would have brought the clothes I bought for you."

"You bought me clothes again?"

"Yeah, but I didn't bring them. You can get them when you come to Port Vista."

Roman tried to parse through his feelings on Demi buying him clothes as he walked to Joss's room. It wasn't enough time. Roman knocked on the door.

TJ opened the door. There was a flush on TJ's neck and face. Silently, TJ stepped aside letting him in.

Joss was pulling on a shirt, a wide grin on his face. "Where's your stuff?"

Roman ignored the scattered love bites and avoided looking at the messy queen bed. "Why would I bring it? I'm not staying with you."

Joss paused then laughed. "You didn't bring me any gifts?"

Roman shifted awkwardly. "Actually I did." He hadn't visited Joss on his birthday like he promised, so to make up for it, he bought him presents. "I forgot to grab them. I'll get them after dinner."

"Good, good, when did you get in?"

"Not long ago, I figured I'd surprise you."

"Alright, alright." Joss clapped his hands. "I'm hungry. Let's get some food."

"I'm starving," Roman said.

"TJ found a place down the street that sounded good."

Ella joined them, and Roman found her refreshing. Roman sat across from Joss and next to Ella. Ella wore a casual dark blue dress with blue eyeliner and her brown hair sat in waves over her tan shoulders.

"Please tell me you aren't going to talk about evobe all night," Ella commented, stirring her soda with a paper straw.

Roman shook his head. "Anything but evobe."

"We have a game tomorrow, what's wrong with—"

Ella boo'd TJ, throwing her napkin at him, her attention shifted to him. "We haven't talked much, tell me about yourself."

"What do you want to know?"

"Which one is better in bed, Casper, Demi, or Joss?"

"I haven't had sex with Joss."

"Hey! Why are you bringing me into it?"

Ella held up her manicured blue nails. "Sorry, I just assumed you had."

"Either way, I'm way better than them," Joss declared, causing the group to laugh.

He separated from the trio after spending two hours with them. He returned to Casper and Demi's room, with the borrowed room key. The door opened, revealing an empty hotel room. Roman changed into comfortable clothes and scooted to the middle of the bed. Settling in he turned on the TV to a show with a marathon of episodes.

Refraining from texting Casper and Demi, it didn't take long for the minutes to pass and soon the door beeped and opened. Demi barely kicked off his shoes before launching onto the bed.

"At least change first," Casper complained from next to the TV, where he was unbuttoning his shirt. "How was dinner with Joss?"

"It was good, Ella and TJ went with us."

"They're buckets of fun," Demi said sarcastically.

Casper came up on his other side, slotting in next to him on his other side. "I'm glad you had a good time."

The next morning, Roman had breakfast with Casper and Demi before they headed out for the game. Roman had another hour before he needed to leave. He hung out in their room until he moseyed out of the hotel and went to the stadium. People flocked in groups, cars lined up for several streets as they entered the parking lot. Roman didn't have a car, so he hobbled the half mile to the stadium. Some fans were already parked and the smell of seasoned shrimp and burgers created enticing tendrils beckoning people closer.

Roman followed the crowd in front of him to the gates of the stadium. Breaking apart as they entered and separately found their seats. Fans trickled in, heading to their seats. He blended in with the Dragons crowd, he wore a shirt that Joss had sent him. He struggled with the steps on the crutches, but he could put a little bit of weight on his leg, just not much. Finally dropping in to his seat, he laid the crutches on the ground. He fiddled with his phone while he waited for the game to begin.

Roman

Good Luck!

Demi

I'm full of good luck ;)

Roman's cheeks flamed, thinking about Demi's good luck blowjob before breakfast. Roman looked through Demi's photogram. There were a few selfies of the three of them. Joss even commented on the post. *Stop trying to steal my best friend.* Demi replied with an emoji with the tongue sticking out.

Roman didn't add to their antics. Instead, he went through Demi's other posts. He was tagged in a few more posts from Demi, a few from winter camp, some from when he stayed over during spring break. He stopped on a post from when they first met at the club. It was a bowl of ramen in his hands from when he took them to his favorite ramen vending machine with the caption... *I could fall for someone who shows me their favorite ramen and buys it for me.* He skipped past it before, since it wasn't a selfie.

He usually only checked Demi's selfies. Roman slid to the next picture and it was Casper and Roman's silhouettes lit up from the vending machine's light. Roman remembered showing Casper his favorites and the ones he didn't like because they were too bland. Casper paid for all of their ramen. Their faces were turned away, so it would be hard to tell who they were. But most of Demi's posts had jokes or some kind of humor to the caption.

Forty-five minutes later, players started to warm up on the field. Runners took shots at the blockers. Demi was in the middle blocker box with Joss on his left, the furthest from where Roman sat. Roman jumped when his shoulder was bumped, too engrossed in watching Casper taking aim at Demi.

Natya grinned next to him. "Did you think I would get you a ticket and leave you here alone?"

"Uh, yes?" That was exactly what he thought.

She sighed dramatically. "Well, that's just not fun for me. Besides, I have to be here to cheer on Thunder so TJ loses. If he wins, he'll annoy me to death with it."

"Right," Roman said. Before the season ended he had gotten just a smidge more comfortable with the team and Natya, but he still never knew how to respond to her. It never mattered because she continued without him.

"You know he's a little goblin. I don't think he's changed. But now he's got a new best friend. Ellie or whatever her name is, which was bad enough, but he's dating Jace or whatever his name is and now he's too good for me."

Roman hummed. The teams were heading to the sideline as the captains met for the coin toss. Thunder won. Roman had noticed that the Dragons always seemed to have terrible luck with the coin toss.

"Rose is good and she's good looking," Natya commented.

Roman saw Naomi Rose on the big screen, she had just gotten five points from Joss. The game continued for every point the Dragons got, Thunder was on them and getting the same point, it was so tit for tat that it almost became predictable.

By the end of the third period everyone was on the edge of their seat to see who would come out on top, tit or tat.

The Dragons won by three points, Roman and Natya jumped from their seats in a cheer, Roman teetered on one leg.

"I thought you weren't rooting for them?" Roman asked.

"Well, I have to root for them if they won!"

Roman shook his head at her logic, the team was jumping up and down on the field gathering around each other. They did it, they were champions. He wished he could be on the field with them next year, to be their teammate but he wouldn't. He swallowed the bittersweet feeling and continued to cheer for his boyfriends and best friend.

27: MAELIE

Roman trudged to his parents' front door, taking a few deep breaths. He was late to the party by over an hour. The outside was decorated extravagantly, they always outdid themselves. He leaned on the crutches for a few seconds before opening the door. The entrance wasn't too different, the only real addition was a draped photo wall covered in little *Maelie's 14th birthday* logos.

The backyard had been transformed with a white tent and a wall of fake diamonds. His parents had made winter come alive in the summer desert heat. Roman stood to the side as the band played. His parents were discussing something near the cake. Maelie was surrounded by her friends, being fawned at. He gained a few glances from the partygoers as he moved through the tables, making his way to his parents.

His mom's eyes lit up. "Romy!"

His dad turned toward him. "You made it," his dad said. He wondered if they doubted he would.

"How about you cut the cake for us?" his mom asked, already handing him the knife.

"Did I miss singing happy birthday?" he asked. "And it's going to be kind of hard." He shifted his arms showing the crutches.

"Oh, no, this is guest cake, what happened to you?"

"I hurt it playing evobe."

"Are you okay?"

"I'm fine."

"Why don't you find a seat? I'll finish this up."

He hobbled his way to the door. Maelie made a production of going on stage. With a shake of his head, he headed back inside.

He stared at the pictures on the wall in the hallway, his were replaced with Maelie's, he wasn't sure if it happened naturally or if they had been switched for the party. In the living room, the family photos were replaced with ones he took, meaning he wasn't in a single photo. Those were purposeful.

Demi

> **How's the party?**

Roman took a selfie of himself alone in the living room.

Roman

> **1 attachment**

> **So much fun.**

Demi

> **Did the party get cancelled?**

Roman took a quick video out of the kitchen window into the backyard.

Roman

> **Attachment sent**

Demi

> **Oh shit. Never mind. Your sister seems popular.**

Roman

> **On even years she has an extravagant party on odd years she goes on a trip.**

Demi

> **Should we have taken you on a trip?**

Roman: My parents don't do it for me. Just for her.

His phone vibrated, Demi was calling him. Roman lifted the phone to his ear after answering it.

"Who the fuck do they think they are?" Demi yelled.

"Calm down," Casper's voice was clearer than Demi's.

"No! I will fucking fuck them up. How dare they! How dare they! Give me my phone, give it to me."

"No, just calm down first. He doesn't need you complaining about his family."

"We'll take him on a fucking trip around the world for his birthday!"

"Dems, Dem, Demi, calm down. He doesn't—stop grabbing at the phone. Knock it off." He could hear rustling and shuffling. "We'll do everything for him. Stop it. I'll fucking kick you if you don't knock it off."

Roman smiled, even if his family didn't care about him, he had his boyfriends. Roman hung up the phone. He wasn't alone anymore.

Casper

> We'll create our own tradition.

He sat in the living room, a place that should feel familiar to him, and yet it was as foreign as a country he had never been to. Carefully, he lifted his leg to stretch out on a cream ottoman. Two hours later, the party guests trickled out, and cleaners and the event planners tore everything down.

"I'm exhausted," his mother said, stepping into the living room. "Romy! I was hoping you were still here. It's been such a hectic day."

Roman mustered up a half smile. "Can I talk to you? Without her around?"

Maelie stood in the doorway, she had changed her outfit since he saw her earlier. She now wore a bejeweled red dress.

"It's my birthday," she whined. "Why can't I stay?"

"Mom, please?" he begged. He just needed one moment without his sister butting in.

195

His mom looked him over, nodded and turned to his sister. "Go on, let me talk to your brother. And no eavesdropping."

Roman waited a few seconds, his mom smiled at him. "What's wrong, sweetie?"

Roman snorted. "Everything, nothing. Why haven't you called or texted me since I left?"

A crease of confusion crossed her face. "I have. You've never responded."

"I haven't gotten anything."

She sighed, pulling out her phone; it took her a few moments before she handed it to him.

He took it and stared at the evidence. None of these messages came through his phone.

Me

How is the summer going?

Happy Birthday!

Happy Thanksgiving!

Merry Christmas!

Are you doing okay? You haven't responded or answered my calls.

Roman?

Please answer the phone.

He hit his contact and stared at an unfamiliar number.

"That's not my number."

"Impossible, I've never changed it."

He snorted. "You probably didn't, but I can guess who did." He fought the urge to scream and yell and throw all the pictures to the ground. Maybe he would have if he hadn't been held back by his leg. "What about my birthdays? You do all of this for her, but what about me?"

His mom sighed. "You never said you wanted a party. You always preferred to stay home and have cake."

"Even the cake, you always chose Maelie's favorite."

"You didn't seem to mind and it saved us from a tantrum."

He crossed his arms. "What about the trips?"

"What about them?" His mom's head tilted.

"You always take Maelie on them."

His mom stared at him, as if studying a puzzle, trying to find the right spot for the piece in her hand.

"I'm sorry," she said. It was low, and she looked at the photos on the wall, her eyes widening.

"Did you just notice I'm not in any of them?"

"Your sister must have done it, another one of her pranks." As if she was a toddler, who still didn't understand the world.

"Mom, I feel like none of you care about me."

She leaned forward, putting a hand on his right knee. "Oh baby, I have never wanted you to feel like that. We may have taken your easy-going attitude as acceptance to her demands. We have always wanted you both to be happy."

He wasn't done though, there was one other thing that bothered him. "What about my college fund?" The money never mattered, he just wanted to know why everything he had went to his sister.

His mom pulled her hand back. "What about it? You didn't need it with your scholarship, it pays for everything. I read through the information on it."

"I lost it. The scholarship." He pointed to his knee. "I lost it, I can't play anymore, I don't want to be in Pennsylvania anymore. I don't know what I'm going to do." His voice cracked. He tightened his fists.

"Sweetie. Do you want to come home? Your room will need to be adjusted again."

His hands clenched in his lap. She was always sidestepping the real issue, focusing on something that didn't matter.

"Mom, you don't even care, not even when I was in the hospital. You never called, you never—" He took in a sharp breath, tears slipping down his cheeks. "You never care about me."

His mom wrapped his arms around him. "I'm so sorry, baby. We didn't know. I really didn't know."

He ducked his head, hands clenched together. "It's all her fault," he whispered.

She pulled back just slightly, to look him in the eye. "Don't blame her."

He yanked away from her embrace. "Things will never change. You will always defend her." His hands splayed out in front of him. "How are you not understanding what she did? How do you just accept all the terrible things she's done to me? I haven't seen you for a year! A YEAR! How do you not care about that?" He stumbled as he stood, picking up the crutches and putting most of his weight on his right foot.

His mom's voice was calm, almost placating as she looked up at him. "Roman, she's your sister, she didn't mean to do anything bad to you, she's—"

"I don't care!" he yelled. He threw down one of the crutches. They both stared at it on the ground. He dipped down and picked it up. "I don't fucking care. I really don't fucking care anymore. How is it so hard to understand?"

"Don't yell at me," she chastised him.

Roman shook his head in disbelief. They could live in their ignorant bliss, no matter what, his sister would always come first. She could murder him and his parents would cover it up.

"I have to go." He made his way to the front door. Maelie was sitting at the top of the stairs not even trying to hide her presence. He couldn't be here anymore, he couldn't listen to his mom take his sister's side anymore. It was ridiculous at this point.

"Roman, wait," his mom called out.

He opened the door and paused just before stepping through. He turned to her. "No, I don't want to hear any more excuses. Why can't you love me as much as you love her?" He threw his arm out, pointing at his sister.

"I do." His mom reached for him, but he stepped back out of her reach.

She wouldn't change, she couldn't because she didn't even realize she treated him differently.

"What about my calls? You never answered them."

"I don't answer numbers I don't know. If it's important I usually get a voicemail."

He wasn't going to leave a voicemail for his mom to call him back. He leaned against the doorway. Staying there to argue about who was right or wrong, was a waste of time. There was no right or wrong, they just stood on two different sides. He saw the sky as red, and she saw the sky as purple. Yelling about it, wasn't going to change what color they saw the sky.

"How about you come over tomorrow? We can talk about it more."

He shook his head. "I have an early flight," he lied. He hadn't even booked a flight yet, but he didn't want to talk to her right now. Not when she wasn't really listening to him.

He walked away from the house, going a few blocks before waiting for a hired car. He leaned on the crutches, staring at the rocks separating the sidewalk and the street. It was the first time he really complained about his sister. The first time he yelled at his mom. The first time he told his mom how he felt. In the end it didn't matter, his mom only cared about his sister.

He was frustrated, he hated that his mom would never take his side. She never asked how or what he was doing. It all felt inevitable, this would have happened at some point in his life. If he had confronted his parents in the garage when they decided to use his college fund for his sister. It might have happened then or when he came home with Casper and Demi in tow.

Knowing something was inevitable didn't stop the pain from blooming in his chest. He rubbed at his face. Nothing was resolved, nothing had been fixed. He basically threw a tantrum and left. He thought he would feel worse, but knowing Casper and Demi were on his side, knowing not just one, but two people loved him. It made the fight feel stupid and childish, but it didn't stop him from feeling disappointed and hurt at his mom's reaction.

As he arrived at the hotel, his mom finally called him. He shuffled to the side, to let others check in.

"Hello?" he answered, without much hope for any resolution.

"I wish you wouldn't have left like that," his mom said.

He set his bag down. "I see you figured out my real number."

His mom sighed. "She had it under spam."

"Of course she did," he muttered. No wonder no one answered or texted him back. "Can we just not talk right now? I'm tired."

"I'll call you later."

"Fine." She could send him an invite in the mail to his sister's birthday party, but it took a year for her to figure out his number was switched only after he told her. Resentment settled deep in his bones.

Roman stared at the ceiling where pounding steps radiated from. He was exhausted after leaving his parents' house. Being in Arizona was lonelier than Pennsylvania. Rolling off of the bed, he quickly grabbed his laptop and looked up flights to Port Vista. He could leave in three hours and be there really early the next morning. The team should be landing soon, so Casper and Demi would be home. Though the hotel was already paid for. By the time he came to a decision it was too late to leave that night. He got a flight for the next morning that would land just past noon.

Roman stood at his parents' door, it was locked so he tried to go around to the side, but it was also locked. He could hear the party and he called out, but no one answered or opened the door. He climbed onto the neighbor's roof. In his parents' backyard, Casper, Demi, and Joss were crowding around his sister like body-guards as people came up to her and bowed at her feet.

He yelled and waved his arms, but they didn't notice him. He stood on the edge of the roof, his foot slipped and he fell to the ground. They finally noticed and surrounded him as he lay on the ground. His sister laughed and then the others laughed. He tried to reach out, but they walked away again, a hole opened up underneath him where he continued to fall.

Roman gasped. Sitting up in the bed, he clenched the sheets to feel something tangible. The hotel room was dark, a faint light filtering through the curtains. It had been a stupid dream.

He reached for the remote on the side table and mindlessly watched TV. The dream and leftover emotions from the confrontation with his mom clung to him like a bad odor. When the sun rose, he got out of bed, gathered up his clothes, brushed his teeth, and left the hotel.

The airport was crowded with business and summer holiday travel. He was surprised to find himself on a full flight. After the layover his flight was only half full and he got an entire row to himself. The closer he go to Port Vista the more his nerves were set on fire. He knew they wanted him there but what if they didn't? He was supposed to go back to Pennsylvania and pack his stuff to leave the dorms. Luckily, he got an extension or he really wouldn't have been able to make it to the game. The new freshman had already started moving in.

He took several deep breaths. He tried to distract himself with a movie Demi recommended, then a book Casper recommended, finally he listened to one of his playlists and allowed his nerves to crash over him. Eventually it would end. The plane would land. He would be on his way to the university and it would be too late to turn back, it would end, he knew that and all the anxiety he was feeling would be a memory. He didn't want to be anxious. He didn't want to be afraid everyone hated him and would leave him if he said something wrong. Anxiety was as natural to him as breathing. It integrated into his life so seamlessly he didn't know when it started or when it affected him, so deeply that he couldn't ignore or get rid of it. Casper and Demi were the perfect distraction.

28: August

He officially lived in Port Vista. He would miss the pink uniforms that now hung in his closet as decorations. The months had gone by in a flash of summer sun, and salty beaches with his boyfriends and Joss, along with physical therapy and calls with his mom.

He was finally moving into his apartment. The apartment was shitty and barely worth the $950 he was paying for it. Gwen had gotten him a part time job at the hot shop, allowing him to pay the rent. It was even smaller than the Dragons dorms, but for now, it was his.

Joss set a box on the kitchen counter. He hadn't needed anything in his dorm, but having his own apartment he needed everything. Demi had gone a little overboard in ordering things. Deliveries had piled up at the door and without being able to return any of it, he couldn't really refuse the gifts.

"When is the food getting here? I'm starving," Joss groaned as he dropped next to TJ on the couch.

"Should be any minute," Roman said, putting silverware away in the small kitchen. It had counter space, but not much space to move around in. Lara came out of the bathroom, joining him in the kitchen as she leaned against the counter. She had flown down to visit and help him move before the semester started.

A few moments later, the door opened. "I've got food," Demi called out.

"And drinks," Ella added, stepping in the apartment behind him with a bag of drinks.

"Finally," Joss said.

"Don't pretend like you're overworked, you moved like two things," Demi said.

Joss stretched out his long legs. "You weren't even here to move one thing."

"I went to get food." Demi shook the four plastic bags in his hands.

"Like that's so hard."

"Then you go next time."

"Can we eat?" Casper cut in, grabbing on of the bags from Demi. "Without all the noise."

Demi scoffed. "He started it."

"Good luck with that, from what I've seen he hasn't been able to shut up," Lara muttered.

Roman bit his lip to stop himself from laughing. Lara was who he would miss the most after moving. He didn't know what the future held, if whatever friendship they had now would fade with time or if they would periodically stay in touch, but whatever it was, he was happy that they had met, had been teammates, were friends. No matter how fleeting it was.

A few hours later, TJ, Ella, Lara, and Joss shuffled out the door. Roman finished putting away the last of his clean clothes in his tiny closet.

Buzz buzz

He grabbed his phone off of his bed, answering it as he put it on speaker and dropped it back to the bed.

"Hi, sweetie, all moved in?" his mom's voice rang through.

"Yeah, just putting stuff away." He adjusted a few glass sculptures on his shelf.

"We'll plan a trip to come see you soon."

He pulled away from the sculptures. "Okay." He was hesitant to agree. He hoped it was an empty suggestion.

"Did you get the money?"

He grabbed a few clean shirts, holding them against his abdomen. "I did. Thank you, you didn't have to help me." He fiddled with the soft fabric. His wardrobe had changed since staying with Casper and Demi. He was starting to wonder if Demi had a shopping addiction because Roman didn't think he needed the amount of clothes that Demi had bought for him. His pink wardrobe was supplemented by an array of colors.

"I'm your mother, of course I'll help you. I'm still sorry about everything."

Roman sighed. They had smoothed over the rough edges, sweeping a few things under the rug, and the rest out the door. He didn't talk about his sister; his mom didn't defend her. It was a teeter-totter, a careful balance of what to say and what not to say. His dad had been easier to talk to, he had asked about his future plans and evobe.

"It's alright," he said. She apologized every time she called, which was now every week, and he continued to tell her it was fine, because it would be. His parents didn't hate him, but he knew they would never care about him the same way they did for his sister. Resentment had simmered into acceptance.

"I still have some stuff to finish up, I'll talk to you next week."

"Goodbye, I love you."

He licked his lips, it was strange that he was more comfortable saying it to Casper and Demi than he did to his own mother. "I love you too. Bye." He watched the phone call end.

Demi knocked on the door frame. "All done?"

"Just finished," Roman said.

Demi held his hand out and Roman entwined their fingers. He led him to the living room where Casper was lighting a candle on top of a lemon cake. He sat on the couch Demi and Casper had in their dorm. Since he refused to allow Casper to buy him a new one, it was donated to him while they got a new one for their dorm.

"You made me a cake?"

"Yeah, I don't know if Casper will want to eat it because I made him taste test as I went. It had to be lemony, but not too sour, but I also didn't want to make it too sweet."

Roman wrapped his arms around Demi, hugging him tightly. "Thank you."

"The cake is going to be waxy soon," Casper reminded them.

Roman turned his head and blew out the candle. This wasn't what he had envisioned for his future, but maybe Joss had been right. Port Vista was where he truly belonged.

ACKNOWLEDGEMENTS

Thank you to everyone who helped make this book come together. Especially my author friends, Val and Minyue.

To my family who continuously support me, especially my husband and dad. This would not be possible without the both of them.

www.ingramcontent.com/pod-product-compliance
Lightning Source LLC
Chambersburg PA
CBHW020410210626
46816CB00006BB/2217